WRITING BY THE SEAT OF MY PANTS

By Raymond F. Quinton

FTNPress
PORTLAND OREGON
© Copyright 2018 Raymond F. Quinton

FTNPress
Publishers Since 1981
2000 NE 42nd, Suite #194
Portland, Oregon 97213
503-933-0120
www.raymondquinton.com
ISBN: 9781549583636

Copyright © 2018 Raymond F. Quinton
All Rights Reserved

OTHER BOOKS BY RAYMOND QUINTON

Afternoon Lunch Guide to San Francisco's Financial District (Restaurant Guide)

The Layperson's Uncensored Relationship Handbook (Self-Help)

Newspaper Carrier Handbook (How-to)

Best Ride Ever! Featuring Oaks Amusement Park (Children's Book)

A Pitch in Crime (Fiction Thriller)

Change the WorkGame (Editor – Workforce Diversity How-to)

Stop Stuffin' Your Pie Hole & Lose Weight Today (Editor)

CONTENTS

Introduction: Write Like A Wang – The Art of 80 WPM - 9
1. The Memory is Fleeting But the Mind is Sound - **17**
2. Liar, Liar Pants On Fire: The Making of a Fibber - **27**
3. I Feel Your Pain: Or,
   Have I Suffered Enough to Be a Great Writer - **33**
4. Write My Son…Till You Drop - **39**
5. Stuff Writers Needs to Know - **47**
6. Everybody's a Writer for Crissakes - **57**
7. Academic Study: Writer vs Kids - **63**
8. It's Chic to be Vague: Or Some, Sommer, Sommest - **69**
9. The Writer's Habitat - **73**
10. Writers and Taxes (Death & Writing) – **79**
11. Wanted: Anyone Who can Write Anything Now! - **97**
12. How To Be a Publisher 101 - **103**
13. Writing In My Sleep - **111**
14. Last Writes or Go Towards the Write – **117**
15. **Epilogue:** Dedication to Calvin Ransom: Kansas 1978 - **121**

PRIMER TO BOOK #1 GENIUS GENES

- (Genius Gene #G1)   Tactical Gene - 8
- (Genius Genes #G2)   Spontaneous Sometimes Erratic Temporary Creativity and Post Scribing - 13
- (Genius Gene #G3)   Unlimited Stress-Anxiety Level Acceptance - 26
- (Genius Gene #G4)   Clever - 30
- (Genius Gene #G5)   Oprah - 39
- (Genius Gene #G6)   Intellectual Improvisation - 53

INTRODUCTION
Type Like a Wang – The Art of 80 WPM

If I were a football team, the fall of 1974 would have been a difficult season for me. I was suffering through my freshman year at St. Xavier's High School in the original distant land of OZ. I was 14, clueless, and desperately trying to reconcile why my parents—after traveling to many far-away exotic places—decided to bring our family of 13 back from France to Junction City, Kansas. Junction City is a place few are from, even fewer ever leave, and even fewer deliberately relocate to. It is a blip on the map of the world, and—to this day—I still miss the exit for it when traveling home to visit my mum. On those occasions, I often—while driving—fall fast asleep right out of Kansas City, Missouri, and wake up somewhere near Salina. I am forced to double-back and apologetically explain to my mum that I missed the exit AGAIN.

Hip-hugger jeans were all the rage. Fashion designers declared that flared pant legs, headbands, vertical striped pants and platform shoes were all good ideas. The next, great world social revolution would emerge with the screening of *Star Wars* at the Hays Valley Mall in Hays, Kansas. And while *Star Wars* took off, Parliament's *Mothership Connection* would land in my best friend Kevin Willmott's Trans Am while we cruised up and down Washington Street. Finally, society would celebrate these events and everything else in discos all over the country.

Seventy-four was also the year I took my first typing class. Through taking that class, I discovered my first, most-important genius gene. This was the first of many genius genes I would eventually discover over the years. I love this gene the most. It is the **Tactical Gene (Genius Gene #G1)**; the mysterious gene of eye-hand, left-brain, right-brain, right-eye, left-eye, left-foot, right-ear, pinky-toe, and right-knee coordination. This is the same gene used to master the piano, ballroom dancing or bus driving. This gene, I believe, is the most complex gene because it manages so many simple things, like, say, typing. As it turned out, this can also be the "trigger" gene that awakens the creato-productive beast within.

Three months into the class, I was typing a phenomenal 80 words per minute; a feat that was not lost on my instructor, Ms. Carolyn Landry. Landry, a soft-spoken, pretty, first-year teacher, drove a 1974 Camaro all the boys thought was bad ass. Her smile could melt butter and calm national unrest, and I privately had a crush on her, which inspired me to over-achieve in her class.

Ms Landry often praised my accomplishments and encouraged me with either a simple "well done Quinton," or, she would find clever ways to "test" my skills. Her goal, it seemed—as I reflect on her teaching technique—was to validate my talents but—at the same time—*not* make things easy for me. She also wanted to instill a sense of humility. Like a Kung Fu master testing her student, she would walk up to my desk, look deep into my soul, then hand me book A through D of the 1974 *Encyclopedia Britannica* and command, "Here, Student Raymond, type the entire contents of this encyclopedia in five minutes. GO!"

"Yes, Ms. Landry," I said, not hesitating to question her request for fear of disapproval.

When Ms. Landry casually turned to walk towards her desk, I cleared my throat and said, confidently, "I am finished Sensei Landry, shall I type it again?"

She turned quickly in my direction. A loud whip-cracking sound echoed throughout the room (like in those 70s martial arts movies), then she squinted her eyes and stared deep into my soul again. With a casual wave of her hand, she said, "dismissed Mr. Quinton." Her attentions immediately focused on other students. "Mr. Peasley?" she announced, "do not pick your nose before you type. It will make your fingers slippery and throw your times off…and your soul will wither like the fallen petals of a rose."

I saw through Ms. Landry's deliberate and deceptive nonchalance. I knew that outside she was distant and dismissive but inside she was jumping up and down and screaming, "WOW, that was outrageous!" There evolved an affinity between Ms. Landry and I. She saw something in me that I did not see. I, after all, was me. It is harder to see yourself than for others to see yourself. Don't ask me to explain. Just think about it. That was all the more reason why it pained me so much to learn years later that Ms. Landry died in a tragic car accident at Milford Lake a few years later.

To this day I have never forgotten the lessons Ms. Landry taught me. Though I type on a fancy laptop now, I could not have gotten here without her gently pushing me to be a better, greater, more compassionate typist. Whenever I prepare to type another story on my fancy laptop, I hear her voice saying—with that same sly, clever nonchalance—"If, Mr. Quinton, you can snatch the Remington Noiseless typewrite from the palm of my hand…" She pauses for effect and I can see her smiling a toothy smile before she continues with, "…before I slap your face, your training will be complete." This was the only exercise I remember questioning because the results were always the same. She held out her palm without a typewriter in it. "Snatch it!" she would command. "There is no typewriter Sensei," I would say. Then she would slap me and say, "you have failed again, now type all 1000 pages of the Southwestern Publishing Company's *Volume Library*...backwards one thousand times in one thousand minutes." That did stress me out a little. No matter. The sound of her voice in my head is still comforting to this say. When I hear the "voice," I must stop what I'm doing, bow my head and whisper to myself, "Yes, Sensei Landry. I am your humble student." Then I shed a silent tear for her. She changed my life.

By my senior year I was FAST! Classmates nicknamed me *Blazing Fingers*. My speeds matched those of an average Wang 1200 Word Processing Unit, and I could out-type even the most experienced and clever corporate secretaries. With skills like that, I *had* to go into journalism; a degree that required massive amounts of typing, writing and ZERO math or chemistry. To top things off, I was obsessed with Clark Kent and Astro Boy, and when choosing a relevant career, timing can make all the difference in the world. So, luck sailed with my career choice and me. *Superman: The Movie* came out in 1978 and made being a reporter *cool* again. I found a great deal of inspiration in the idea of being a journalist/superhero. I could disguise myself as a mild-mannered American Negro/superhero/reporter who could type bad guys to death. I've been living incognito ever since.

Before I could take on that awesome responsibility, however, I still had three more years of high school and four years of college to get past. During those seven years, there were important questions I needed to answer before embarking on my super-hero-journalist professional career. The answers to these questions would play an integral role in defining my future pathways and influencing the contents of this book.

Some of questions I asked are as follows:

- Does it take great intellect to type fast?
- Was typing going to be my super power?
- Was the rate at which I typed any measure of my creative capacity?
- If I were indeed a fast-typing super hero, would I also be a super writer? I mean, would I have to super deal with rejection letters, or would I fly through the window of the publisher's who sent the offending rejection letter and super-ask, "why do you think my crime novel super sucks?"
- How fast do great writers need to type…if using a typewriter? If no typewriter was available, how fast could they quill?

- Physics questions: How fast can you type before the keyboard becomes superheated, bursts into flames, and causes time to go backwards?
- Is the speed of typing directly equated to intellectual acumen?
- Oh, and who is an intellectual anyway? Will I know one when I see one?

Through asking questions and challenging what I thought I knew, I discovered some obvious answers. Other questions, however, begged further exploration. I've always had the gritty, survivalist spirit of the earlier Kansas pioneers *and* my Jamaican Maroon ancestors, so I approached writing as a survival skill, like skinning beavers for food and clothing or raiding slave plantations for guns and supplies. Some write to show how smart they are. Others write because they have a lot of time. Writing has always fed me, spiritually and physically. You can't eat words, but you can write a paragraph you think is fantastic then charge everyone you know a dollar to read it. Suddenly you don't *just* have words. You've got food.

So, let's cut to the chase. This is a book of exploration of my ideas. It is a glimpse into the bizarre thing that was and is my writing slash "other" career. I don't consider this the crowning achievement of my illustrious career as a writer super hero (a.k.a. Blazing Fingers). It is simply the current stark raving ramblings and semi-intellectual processing about a career out of control. While I've got the podium, I don't hesitate to explore culture, race, music and love.

I've written a little of almost everything and a lot of some things. I played Mr. Scott in *Star Trek the Musical* in college and wrote the radio script for *Savage Senior Citizens*. I've lunched with the late, fabulous Barbara Tropp (whom I adored), Wolfgang Puck and Jeremiah Tower in San Francisco. I've chatted with Jan Wiener at *Rolling Stone* headquarters and Hugh Sidey at Time Inc. headquarters in New York. I even opened for Dizzy Gillespie at Union Station in Denver. In 2016—while applying for my Jamaican Passport in New York City—I attended a reception at *Fast Company* headquarters for former American Society of Magazine Editors interns at 7 World Trade Center. Many of the top editors in New York were there…and so was I. I've published upwards to 10 magazines; seven books and written and published millions of words. My brush with real minor fame came early with my first book, *The Afternoon Guide to Lunch in San Francisco's Financial District*, and fame scared the hell out of me. So I retreated quickly and decided that while I appreciate fame, it has a way of taking over a person's life and changing their brain chemistry. I preferred to operate behind the scenes. So, with my partner, Drew Patterson, I founded the Guide Publishing Group (*Bay City Guide*) in San Francisco and pushed forward as an accomplished editor and publisher in San Francisco, Portland and Seattle.

The funny thing about my career is…I've been able to maintain my disguise. I feel like I've been living some weird Forestgumpish illusionary life. I'm not a rock star, but I've found myself in the company of some of the most amazing people around. I feel like a voyeur sometimes. In 1980 I met Mayor Koch in New York as he christened in a new fleet of buses in Brooklyn. I tripped over Art Blakey in London while he performed with my cousin's band members. The list of these acquaintances, encounters and experiences goes on and on. Meanwhile, I actually view myself as a simple (perhaps simple-minded) observer, and a humble, professional wordsmith, journalist, publisher, and editor. I've also formulated some close friendships with some really nice people and marinated some outrageous theories and ideas. What's that old saying? I'm now old enough to have clear opinions and not afraid to use them. As I tour with this book, I'll be able to have conversations about these experiences and you'll read about some of them in this book.

There are books on writers. There are books about writing. There are books about writers writing about books on writers. There are books about writers thinking about writing books about writers writing books on writing. Most of these books are collecting dust on bookshelves everywhere. The real meat of writing I believe lies in the quest to discover why so many writers are obnoxious big fat liars and what the point of writing really is. I contend that most great writers would rather be doing things other than writing, like building stuff or operating cranes. The process of writing is like having an extended orgasm. It's mentally exhausting but hard to *classify* as real work. That's why there's so much writer envy out there. If you could have an eight-hour orgasm, would you? I also dig deep into the underworld of writing. The pleasure. The pain. The Joy. The Angst. The weirdness. I cover all THAT stuff from my bizarre semi-intellectual perspective, which is *the* most important perspective. At the same time, I'm having fun with words and style.

I also introduce the concept that every individual has multiple **genius genes** as opposed to the common theory that people are either a genius or *not*. Our real challenge as humans is to figure out which genius genes we have and how to harness them and use them in various combinations to affect a better world and a better life. To start the process, I have identified the various genius genes in this book, and will identify more in the subsequent two-book installments.

If you want to be a writer, don't just say you want to be a writer. WRITE! Words are the most important tools we have as an "advanced" society. If you're not using them every day to effectively communicate ideas, you're wasting our time. I'm 58 years old, and I have used words to positively impact every aspect of my life, my community, my relationships and my craft. For my wife's birthday, I wrote her a tiny, super-short, super-romantic novel. It was funny, romantic and brought both of us great joy. We, of course, were the main characters in the book.

This book is an extension of my effort to change the world with words. As I tour and do readings, I'll advocate for people to NOT wait until they retire or have some *free* time to write anything useful. Tomorrow you could be dead. Write NOW! Communicate NOW! Change the world NOW! If you can write, WRITE RIGHT AWAY! There is an urgent need. Society needs your skills NOW! It's frustrating for me to hear people say, "Now that I'm retired I think I'll do a little writing." I've been writing most of my life and trying to make the world a better place. I've had to hustle and be incredibly clever at times. I find it incredibly difficult to sit around listening to people casually talking about going to the beach or the cabin or the second home and doing a little writing for the last 20 years of their lives. I see that weird blank look awash their faces; that look that says, "I'm smart. I've got a pension. I'm comfortable. I no longer need to continue the struggle to better society. Nor do I need to interact with people not like me. I can live in my head. I can have an eight hour orgasm EVERY day." Writing becomes an end-of-life ritual, and that makes me sad.

Yes, I concede that writing can be revealing, therapeutic, relaxing and can be used to entertain as well. That's important. But I also believe that writing and human interaction are a vital combination. For example, I wrote my first children's book so I could spend time reading it to kids. It's selling well, in most of the libraries in the area, but I could care less whether I sell a million copies. Reading my book to over 100 kids during Portland's Park and Rec's summer free lunch in the park program was the most gratifying experience of my entire career. That's what makes it all worth it. That's why I'm looking forward to embarking on my *Party Like a Writer - Half World Tour*. Writing is easy. Talking to people is hard. The great thing about being in disguise as a Negro writer-superhero is knowing that I can save the world and still be a normal person when I get home.

The other great thing about being a writer is that if you're bold enough to write it, it must be right!

Let's get on with it shall we? Enjoy. Write often! Live More! Proclamation! Exclamation! Ad Infinitum!

Chapter 1
The Memory is Fleeting But the Mind is Sound

We writers are cursed, in many ways, from the day we decide to write for a living. Our tools are words, symbols, punctuation and lots of complicated grammatical rules. We use these tools to craft sentences, create imagery, scribe life, and tell stories. To write well, we must call on all of our creative faculties, instincts, training, experiences, imagination, and that collective, creative consciousness many talk to create prose *others* might be interested in reading—or, perhaps, even be inspired to action by. Writing is an awesome task and a formidable, exacting process. I could stop there. But NO! Many writers feel it is their responsibility to write to save the world. And, for taking on this daunting responsibility, some writers—at the end of the day—even expect to be paid for their intellectually creative acrobatics, like the revered members of Cirque Du Soliel.

I have toiled like a blacksmith tempering sentences to perfection and forging prose to paper. Once done, I allowed my words to cure into paragraphs, then I molded and tooled those paragraphs into pages, chapters, and even large blocks or volumes of words on paper known as books. Thoughts scribed. Meanings expressed. Mission accomplished? Yes? Maybe? Perhaps not. Um, uh, I don't remember!!!!!!!! I *can't* remember. Did yesterday happen yesterday or the day before? Where did all those words go and did I really write them? What can or do we really remember? Why can't I remember anything I've written?

Some men and women are endowed with the genius gene of perfect, exact recall. Some rely heavily on notes. Others, like me, are doomed to rely on the ficklest of the **Genius Genes, #G2 (G2 -** ***Spontaneous—Sometimes Erratic Temporary Creativity and Post Scribing Amnesia*)**. This genius gene impacts memory, and—according to top researchers—is possibly influenced by one or more traumatic childhood mishaps. My siblings held the key to my first *possible* traumatic childhood event. They claimed that while our family was living on a country estate in France with a poodle named Pierre, I one day reached into my diaper, wrapped my fingers around a fresh turd blossom, yanked it out and proceeded to eat it. Thus, the term shit-eating grin was born into the world of the baby Raymond. For now, we must set aside the fact that both my legs were in corrective casts, the result of a birth-based bone deformity. I'll talk more about that in another book. For now we'll focus on this question: Is eating your own shit cause for lingering childhood trauma? Maybe? But please monsieur and mademoiselle allow me to explain.

The family rumor mill has it that some of my older brothers and sisters found me that day. (*Disclaimer: This is not a lie.*) Since I'm the eleventh child out of 13 siblings, my older brothers and sisters—some in their teens—remember this unfortunate event vividly. Me? I remember nothing about it.

As the story goes, it was France, nineteen hundred sixty something or the other. Apparently, I allegedly reached around, grabbed a recently manufactured turd nugget out of my diaper and had lunch—again. I don't remember that. Would you?

During holidays some siblings were not shy about regurgitating this event whenever they were sure *I* was in the room AND there was a captive audience of family. Out of the corner of the table, one of my older siblings would shout over the turkey, "Hey, Raymond, do you remember when you ate your own shit?!"

The story was always the same and always drew spontaneous applause and aghast. I vehemently disputed and denied the memory. Were these true or false memories? Was it really France? Are there any pictures? My immediate response was that I remember France vividly, "but I don't remember eating my own shit. We were all very young," I claimed.

Embarrassed, I stood up and yelled, "Maybe *you* ate *my* shit!" In frustration I also proclaimed, "If you'll excuse me, I have to go to the bathroom." That only brought on more laughter and sniggers. That, however, was my only way out—leaving the table immediately to take refuge in the bathroom. The bathroom was the only room in our ancient Junction City family home with a door that could lock from the inside. I was safe there.

Those traumatic family experiences helped evolve a sophisticated selective memory defense mechanism. It seemed a convenient tool; a safety net of sorts, and I seemed to have some natural talent for it. I began refining this skill early on. The key to genius genes is to recognize them and learn to exploit them for the good of humanity. My goal was to master this ridiculous gene. Part of that mastery involved reading a lot of Erich Fromm. From those readings I evolved the idea that memory can be a burden or a benefit. Memory, after all, can be dense and heavy like lead or soft, malleable and valuable like gold.

While I eventually mastered the aforementioned skills, I also have vivid recollections of exercising the burgeoning ability of deliberate memory lapse in third grade. It was spring in Kansas. Or, was it winter? Crap, I don't fucking remember. I do remember that I was curious about love and I didn't want to be called a "good nigger" any more by my classmates.

For effect, let's settle on the idea that it was spring. I had a massive crush on Viki VanSchmedermeir (name changed to protect the innocent). She was a very pretty blonde with bright blue eyes and a really cute laugh. I was the only Negro in my class, and she was the only girl in class who seemed even remotely interested in being my girlfriend. The other girls didn't talk to me much. They were quietly being told at home to "stick with your own." In 1968, there was a tenuous peace between blacks and whites at St. Xavier's School. In another part of the world the Vietnam war was escalating and cities all over the country were burning due to racial unrest. Junction City was a weird multicultural bubble, populated by diverse military families, farmers, retired veterans and immigrants from all over the world. We were one of two large Negro families in the school. My seven older brothers were fine athletes and most of my sisters were all brilliant academically. Mom dressed us all up and took us to church every Sunday. Monsignor Thomas Keogan, a dynamic Irishman who flung spit bombs when he talked with his thick Irish accent, was pleased with us. The word on the Catholic streets of Junction City was, "Don't mess with the Quintons." Most of my classmates were from farming families who complained about "the niggers" at home, but were almost civil to our family in school and around town. I say almost because this school was not the insulated, safe environment that it seemed. My classmate's real views spilled out regularly when the priest and nuns were busy praying or parading around in costumes and waving incense in the air. Some of my classmates loved to use words like "nigger," "coon," "spear-chucker," and popular, regional, cultural environmental ethnic terms like "jungle bunny," "sand nigger," "towel-head," "beaners," and the one I *never* really understood, "nigger-lipping."

I love all things romantic, but growing up in a small town in Kansas—if you're a Negro—was NOT romantic. My only shelter was George Smith Public Library, which was a block away from our house and a place I considered my second home. There, I lived in my own fantasy world (similar to *World of Warcraft*) fed by books about nature, Greek Gods, and far-away places. The library helped me maintain optimism, a romantic outlook on life, and sheltered me from the daily racial stress and Monsignor's spit bombs.

I would not give up on my romantic ideals no mater what. In school I believed that maybe Viki could love me, even though I felt the constant racial micro-hostilities around me. When all the other girls and boys would play "sandwich" and chase down a girl and a boy and push them together (like a sandwich) on the playground, I was never selected. Nor were the fat kids, the nerds, or smart kids. I was part of a distinctive class of outsiders. I thought that maybe Viki could see me as a human being, not as the manifestation of the terribly, stereotypical Negro imagery my classmates and their families to so they could preserve their way of life. I was a boy not the bogeyman. Maybe there would be a major break through. Maybe I could be more than just the nigger black kid in the class. Maybe I could be the major love interest of one of the prettiest girls in the school…just like Mickey Rooney (Yes, I saw every movie). He danced. He sang. He always got the girl.

Okay, my penchant for optimism started early. Keep in mind that I was still a classic, naïve, dumb kid. I had not studied philosophy and psychology yet. That was still years away. I had not reached the age of enlightenment. I just wanted to figure out the love and romance thing. The movie people said it's supposed to be really GREAT. White people fell in love in the movies while the black people were shown dancing around fires in the jungle serving white people and working on trains as porters. Hey, I'm a child of the media. Cut me some slack. I tried to blank out the racist, negative imagery in the movies and opted to embrace the optimism of White culture. That prompted my next move.

One day I decided to write a love note to Viki. If I could deliver this note—like the heroes in the movies—Viki would love me. She would see the genius in my prose, and she would see past my skin color. We would fall in love, and we would sing *Our Love is Here to Stay* (like Gene Kelly & Leslie Caron in *An American In Paris*) in the playground at recess. The only complex decision that day was to decide how to deliver the note efficiently to her.

The method I settled on was to fling the communiqué three rows over in hopes it would land squarely on Viki's desk. Unfortunately, Sister Mary Magdalene was a master note interceptor. While she wrote the word of the day on the board, I balanced the paper square upright on my desk with my index finger, pointed it in Viki's direction, cocked my other finger and flicked the note in Viki's direction. Sister Magdalene's nun senses were on high alert. As the white, tightly folded note-square flew over David Peasley's head and fell to the floor next to Viki, Sister Magdalene turned and spotted the note on the floor. It sat in the isle like a flashing red emergency beacon on a fire truck. Her eyes darted from the note to me, and I might as well have been standing in the isle with a protest sign that read, I THREW THE NOTE! PLEASE DON'T DO WHATEVER IT IS YOU'RE THINKING ABOUT DOING!

"Bring that to me right now, Quinton," she said, not blinking or ruffling any of the neatly carved rivers of wrinkles on her face.

All eyes were on me as I stood, slid from behind my desk, shuffled up the isle, fetched the note, and slowly walked it to the front of the classroom. I averted my eyes. It is forbidden to look into a nun's eyes when you get that close. Come to think of it, I don't remember looking into a nun's eyes from a distance. They were not human, after all. They were God's servants, and the *habit* was an intimidating aperture not to a human but to an entity. I placed the note in Sister Magdalene's ancient, blotched, slightly shaking hand. Eyes still averted, a halo of shame floating over my head, I returned to my desk.

There was silence as Sister Magdalene read the note. Then, she cleared here throat and began to read it again out loud to the class.

When she finished reading, the laughter was like a looping laugh track from a bad sitcom. I slumped down in my seat and tried, like a superhero, to will myself invisible.

"Silence everyone!" Sister Magdalene commanded. Laughter stopped immediately as if a producer had pushed a button marked MUTE DUMB KID LAUGHTER.

"Quinton, did you write this?" She asked sternly, while furrowing her forehead, which created a forehead wrinkle tsunami.

Sweat flowed freely from every available orifice on my body. My mind went blank. I pressed my eyes closed and pushed the memory of the note down as far as I could. Then, my eyes suddenly opened wide and there, before me, was a bright light where Sister Magdalene was standing. Jesus was standing next to her, whispering something in here ear then covering his mouth and sniggering. It was all clear to me. First, the word "snigger" was too close to another offensive word I was very familiar with. Next, I no longer remembered writing the note. Instant, spontaneous amnesia. I was at peace as Sister Magdalene continued reading the note with Jesus watching and sniggering the entire time. The note read as follows:

Dear Viki,

I really like your shoes today. You also smell good. Are you wearing perfume? David said you don't like him anymore. Is that true? Should I stop being his friend now? What are you doing at recess? My dad made me wear really big pants today. I can't run too fast or they'll fall down. Hey, will you marry me?

Raymond

I remember staring off into space. When I finally became aware of my surroundings again, I was 25 years old, haunted by the trauma of that experience but profoundly aware that Sister Magdalene and the sniggering Jesus had done me a favor. Viki received a life sentence in jail—a victim of the Kansas three-strikes legislation—and I was navigating an already complex publishing career.

As I grew older, I, like Hemingway, became a copious communicator, never lacking thoughts or words to use to describe them. My letters were often 10-page diatribes about the wonders of anything; social theory, psychological prognosticating, and good old problem solving. My friends loved me because I was willing to patiently listen to *them* talk about whatever they wanted to talk about. After all, my brain was unburdened by the minutia of workaday banter and memory. If a friend had issues with a scuff on a new pair of shoes, my response was, "Well, tell me about that. How does that make you feel?" Voila, instant best friend. Lurking in the memory background of my gradual rise, however, was a plump little black baby lying in a crib nibbling on a turd nugget. I was banging on the sides of the crib with my crippled, cast-wrapped legs, while Sister Magdalene stared down at me as she listened intently to Jesus whispering something in here ear about you-know-who and sniggering uncontrollably. The genius of selective forgetting was more refined, but that skill presented other social challenges for me, especially anything pertaining to any written communications.

I became quite paranoid and insecure about this skill, and—in an attempt to find balance and mindfulness—I developed the habit of copying all written correspondence before sending them to anyone. I copied *everything*. I even copied Post-It notes. I copied my graffiti. For example, if I wrote "Here I sit all broken hearted, tried to shit but only farted," on a bathroom stall wall, I would scribble a reminder note on some toilet paper and file it. Fortunately, my first real job out of college was as a corporate librarian in Denver, so I had the chops to Dewey decimal the hell out of what was becoming an elaborate library of my correspondence.

I created files for every letter I wrote. I sorted and filed them in chronologically order *and* cross-referenced them alphabetically. I had a system, and that system worked incredibly well for a while, with some noticeable snags. The snags often happened when a friend called after receiving a letter from me and wanted to talk about the contents. Immediately Sister Magdalene and the sniggering Jesus would flood my brain and I would freeze up. The silence on my end of the phone was sometimes deafening. When this happened, I was forced to get quite creative about retrieving relevant information to further the conversations. My Ninja corporate librarian training kicked in and I sprang into action. I wasn't deceptive. Nor was I dishonest. I was a man of action with a defective genius gene.

If said friend on the phone and I reached a point in the conversation where something I wrote was mentioned and I couldn't remember what the heck it was, I abruptly announced, "Can you hold on for a second, my living room is on fire and I've got to go put it out."

That allowed for unlimited time to go to my research/reading library—which included mini-microfiche cabinets, a photo library and periodicals reading room for my first zine, *Rabid City Humor Magazine*. I could find the reference, check it out from my library (tolerate sideways glances from the librarian...questioning my choice of reading materials), then I could conclude the call, return the materials to my library, and avoid any fines. Mission accomplished. Friendship disaster averted.

If I was at a dinner party and the same scenario presented itself, I simply announced, "I forgot to put the laundry in the dryer. I'm going to go home. Be back soon. Ta-Ta. Auf Viedersehen. Thank you for shopping!"

I'd drive home, retrieve and review the relevant documents, then return to the dinner party and continue the conversation as if I never left.

"Oh, what I meant was that some psychosis are directly related to the prime interest rate. It's called HOMPS, home mortgage paranoia syndrome and thank you for the lovely evening."

"We finished talking about that two hours ago, Raymond," my host would politely remind me. I'd smile and simply say, "Scrabble anyone?" Once again, I later returned the documents to the library without incurring any late fees and avoiding the librarian's wrath.

I began to suspect, too, that my inability to remember what I wrote was a psychological disclaimer and an indictment of my profession; a message from deep inside reminding me that when I write, I mostly make stuff up. Reminding me that writing may not be real work. Reminding me that maybe I needed to build a house or something to validate my existence.

Was I alone in feeling this way? Or, were there other writers going through this same thing? Over the years I also learned there *were* writers with tremendous capacities to remember stuff. You know the type; those people who can quote Shakespeare after reading a rather lengthy piece only one time. I'm very concerned about those people. Doesn't storing all those words hurt? OR—and I have nightmares about this one—did Sister Magdalene and the sniggering Jesus put a Catholic hex on me after I blanked out?

Whatever the case, I had to convince myself that this was a puzzle I might *not* want to solve; an affliction that could, in fact, be a great asset some day, especially if I ever decide to go into politics. Everyone knows, after all, that the inherent risk of being a politician is that you could someday wake up to find yourself testifying before some committee or the other about something written in a letter to a friend many years earlier. That friend, coincidentally, becomes a radical conservative revolutionary obsessed with all that is conservative (clothes, books, cars, writing utensils, you know the type) and wants to overthrow the United States government and convert it into 52 independent nations—one new one being named after him or her.

If I should find myself in Congress, for example, as a senior senator sitting in the hot seat of a congressional hearing, I would conjure up a smug look of superiority and calm. My esteemed colleague would stare down at me. He would be drooling at the prospect of catching me—perhaps the nation's most popular public figure—in a big fat lie. I would match his stare, toke on my cigar, prop my cowboy boots up on the table, cut lose a confident, mischievous Brad Pitt grin and say, "take your best shot, senator."

"Senator Quinton, in this letter to Bob Simmons—who calls himself the rightful King of the United States and heir to the throne of the world—you write—and I'll quote—'if I ever make it to the senate, I'll finally be in a good position to help you overthrow the government of the United States.'" He holds up the letter and waves it around and enters it into the official transcript then turns to me, lowers his glasses and asks, "What do you have to say for yourself Senator Quinton?"

Composed, cool, collected, I'd first wink into the cameras, spit a wad of chaw on the floor, squint, and say in my most impressive Dirty Harry tone, "Senator, I forgot to put the laundry in the dryer." Then I'd get up and run from the room, never to be seen again.

Chapter 2
Liar, Liar Pants On Fire: The Making of a Fibber

It's no secret that writers all over the world suffer from a terrible disease. As most people settle into their comfortable domiciles for the evening, writers worldwide are sitting on plain metal folding chairs in semi-circles around stone-faced counselors in dark, dingy independent bookstore basements. They're taking turns saying—between suppressed sobs—"My name is Soandso and I'm a writer. I lie like a rug and I am powerless to stop."

To make matters worse, there seems to be a concurrent pandemic-level outbreak of writers everywhere, further fueling the spread of their occupation-specific affliction. In an attempt to get ahead of this problem, researchers at Kansas State University's bovine genetics research lab are conducting research to find a solution to this problem. They hope to identify writers through DNA screening. If they are successful, then, well, you know what they'll have to do? I'm going to go ahead and say this because there's no politically correct way to put it. They'll—well—um, uh, they'll need to euthanize the contributing parent to eliminate the risk of more diseased writers being produced in our society.

Fortunately, the bovine research lab is behind in their research and we are not living a dystopian future where genetic writer-engineering is perfected, so we must live with the fact that more writers will still be born unto the world. Social media will continue to expand access and opportunities for liar-writers, and our writer-plagued world will continue on its current course.

NOW, let me inject a positive note about writers at this juncture. I don't want people to get the wrong impression and believe that writers deceive or con others deliberately. They are not habitual, pathological criminals. They are victims of their occupation *and* genetic pre-determination. The very nature of their work requires them to issue false preverifications (my word) wherever convenient. In plain King's English—as my Jamaican grandmother Gregg used to say—they must "lie, lie, lie mon."

To further expound on this social phenomenon a little further, let me provide context with a technical definition of a writer. Below is the *American Heritage* definition of a writer. Please note that I've taken some creative license and abridged the definition with my personal notes.

WRITER DEFINITIONS

Writing:

1. To lie (letters, words, or symbols) on a surface such as paper with an instrument such as a liar's pen.
2. To form lies (letters or words) in cursive style (an archaic artistic form of lyin').
3. To lie, especially in literary or musical form.
4. To fib in legal form; draft.
5. To fill in or cover with lies.
6. To lie in writing; set down.
7. To lie by correspondence.
8. To underwrite lies, as an insurance policy.
9. To depict lies clearly; mark.
10. To ordain or prophesy (lie).
11. Computer Science. To lie (with data) on a storage device.
12. To produce written lies, such as articles or books.
13. To compose a lie; communicate lies by mail.

That's just for starters. The *Roget's Thesaurus* reveals the following about writing:

Writing as a Noun: *An untrue declaration. Story, fiction, tale, falsehood, falsity, misrepresentation, untruth, whopper, canard, fib, misstatement, prevarication.*

At this juncture, I should rest my case, but there are a few important points I simply *must* make. My favorite word in the above citation above is *whopper*. This word seems to most appropriately define what writer do. Writers who managed to profit from telling the most outrageous whoppers, are the ones who have turned their disability and disease into a career.

If you think the views I hold are totally unfounded, I will tell you I've done my research on this subject. I've even searched the archives at Harvard, made numerous inquiries on the Internet, and, finally, talked to an aging Midwesterner named Marvin Neidermeyer. Neidermeyer confirmed that the first story ever told by the first writer on earth was the result of a big fat lie; a lie created out of shear desperation.

Neidermeyer, a warm-hearted, unassuming, embodiment of Midwestern values, who lived an austere life in La Cross, Kansas, once possessed an ancient scroll containing the first colossal fib. He bought it at a junk store for a dollar. World famous archeologist, Sterdevant Van Eggmont apparently uncovered the scroll during an archeological expedition in Algeria. After he found it, he spent the next 25 years of his life translating the Sanskrit symbols, interpreting the hieroglyphics, and discovered the ancient story of *The One That Got Away*.

After he finished translating the scroll, he sent it, along with his copious notes, to the Museum of Man and Mice in Scranton, Ohio, for safekeeping.

The scroll and the notes never made it.

Evidently, the UPS driver who picked up the package had a heart attack and crashed the delivery truck before reaching the museum. The scroll popped out of the truck, and, um, uh, went right down the chimney of a nearby house. The owner of the house, a local junk dealer, Piedmont Burgenballer, found the scroll and the notes and sealed them in a framed macramé of a John Deer Waterloo Boy tractor. He then hung the macramé in his store. There it hung for another 37 years until Neidermeyer bought the framed macramé for a dollar at a going-out-of-business sale. He thought the macramé was brilliant, but he actually wanted to use the frame for a macramé picture of a red New England barn in fall. Neidermeyer was not sure what he had discovered behind the macramé, but once he started reading, his face froze in a look of horror and dismay for two weeks. This caused a problem when he made love to his wife.

Neidermeyer discovered the truth about writers. The scroll described an ancient hunter, who, while foraging for sustenance, encounters a critter with seventeen eyes, six feet, and looked sort of like a giant rat with some problematic genetic lineage. The hunter describes how he chased the agile beast for 16 hours before it dove into a cave and escaped. In an inconspicuous footnote, however, the hunter admits that he made the whole story up rather than experience the shame of returning home to his brood without even so much as a Etruscan shrew for vittles. In truth, he actually spent the day napping on a cliff overlooking the valley and dreaming about better, simpler times; times when humans widely adopted vegetarianism and didn't have to hunt scary, dangerous beasties.

Harvard scholar, Peter Goldschmidt, heard of the find and immediately went to La Cross, where he confirmed the scroll's authenticity and purchased it for one hundred million dollars CASH. Goldschmidt further confirmed that the scroll did indeed contain an outrageous lie and confession; a lie that has manifested, and replicated over thousands of years. Unfortunately, each time the story was told, it became more outrageous. The story was so outrageous that today it is consider unequivocally factual. Through numerous studies and more queries on the Internet, it was ascertained that this story actually inspired many famous writers, such as James Baldwin, John Gresham, Stephen King, and Dean R. Kontz, to name a few. All, have become rather astute, incredible liars by studying this ancient scroll and exploiting its secret.

Those who read the scroll affirm the birth of fiction. Fiction, of course, is the most elaborate, documented telling of tall tales. It seems that many societies celebrate fiction and have even evolved a dependency on the conveyors of poppycock. They even go so far as to encourage the creation of such by paying authors millions of dollars to simply lie to their heart's content.

Consider, for example, the proposal for a science fiction novel. It is, by all rights, nothing more that an elaborate means of telling a publisher you're thinking about telling a prodigious tale. On top of that, you're asking said publisher to pay you handsomely for this potential lie. I will admit that I've been paid quite well to write proposals that involve the legitimate selling of services. That seems reasonable and a valid quid pro quo. The fiction proposal, however, asserts something entirely different; that a tremendous lie will eventually be told, and that payment should be forthcoming—and in spades—before AND after the canard is actually told. I'm concerned about that paradigm.

It would not be fair, of course, to label all writers *hopeless* liars. That was my hook, but I assert that much of the writing that's valued today is some form of embellishment on some non-or half-truth, and we've come to thrive on it. I don't have a serious problem with that. I would simply like all of us to be a little more forthcoming about what writing—particularly fiction—really is. I would like us to stop using the word *fiction* to dress up the dubious activity of lyin'. I would like us to stop using the word "creative" to give incredible fibbing credence. We writers are liars, and our pants are on fire like a burning Viking funeral ship. We must acknowledge that fact. Lastly, I'd like to see the title of the *New York Times* best-selling fiction list changed to The *New York Times* best-selling *liars'* list. Than—and only then—will we be a truly free society, a society with a happy inner child, and a society that can one day be comfortable with itself and it's ability to lie. Then—and only then—will the fire in our pants be doused and the writer-liar disease abolished from earth forever.

Chapter 3
I Feel Your Pain:
Or, Have I Suffered Enough to Be a Great Writer

As a writer, I often wondered whether I suffered enough to be a really *great* writer. During the early years of my career I had achieved great speed. I had earned my *Golden Inverted Pyramid Journalist* pin. I achieved the distinguished title of publisher six months out of college. By that time I—in my humble opinion—had not really suffered any physical pain outside of spankings, minor football injuries and a broken heart. All mendible. I was a pensive person, so I thought incessantly about whether I was worthy of success if I was having a lot of fun and experiencing very little pain and suffering.

To address the aforementioned question, I devised the *pain-quotient theory*. It goes something like this. To be a great writer, the pain I suffer must be the "right" kind of pain to inspire the "right" kind of creativity. For example, is a hangover the "right" kind of suffering? Perhaps. Perhaps not. Yes, my friends, these are the crazy kinds of musing that flowed through my head while eating meatball sandwiches near the Plaza in Kansas City, napping in The park at Michigan State University, jogging in Queensboro Park or while eating curry at an Indian restaurant in London.

I flittered like a butterfly through my life from one crazy career situation to the other, never really looking back to measure my pain and suffering quotient accurately. While on my self-imposed sabbatical in London in 1985, I promised myself that if later on in my life I determined that I was "pain" deficient, I might need to do something drastic to remedy that situation. With the right kind of pain, I surmised, I would be able to reach a level of creativity yet to be reach by any writer on earth. Pain would be my creative catalyst, and if I couldn't find it organically, I would find a way manufacture it.

Well, later turned into 1995, my friends, and the pain deficiency was real. There was suffering all around me. Dessert storm. Unemployment. Crack cocaine. All sorts of terrible things. There was pain all around me, but I wasn't getting any of it. My pain depravation ultimately gave in to desperation. Thus, with incontrovertible reasoning in mind, I decided to make the noble gesture of offering up my nut sack to the gods of pain. I would allow them to be cut open and have a hot soldering iron inserted into them. I would experience unimaginable pain AND humiliation. In exchange, I could earn my writer's *Massive Amounts of Pain and Suffering & Deep Personal Sense of Loss Pin*. This experience would make me a better writer. This notion fed my next genius gene, **Genius Gene #G3. (G3: Unlimited Stress-Anxiety Level Acceptance).**

I think I heard you say, "Yikes! Where did that come from?" Houston, this is Writepollo 13, we do have a story-telling problem?

How did we get from creative pain to testicular pain? Allow me to connect the dots. At the writing of this story, my then and future x-wife had gone through the pain and agony of bearing our two children. The first child almost killed her, and the second child, born via emergency cesarean, almost died and killed her again. I was a good husband and while I was there, I, for the most part, was a pain-free participant. There was some emotional pain, but nothing I could really say OUCH! to.

Everybody in my household had suffered, I stood, defiantly, on an island of non-suffering. I began writing this book around that time, but I was too happy; definitely NOT feeling like I had suffered enough. The only noble alternative for me, I thought, was to share in that suffering; find a way to sacrifice a few little chunks of myself for the better of the whole, to serve the needs of the many, at the expense of the few, the one.

So, after much emotional wrangling, I, with the blessings of my wife, decided to have a vasectomy. OOORAAH! Semperfidelis! Bring on the pain, I thought. The journey began in earnest. I did my homework. I read as much as I could, saw the video, signed the papers, and made the appointment. I was excited, but I also, for the next month, quietly agonized about the tremendous amount of pain I would endure. I thought, "I am going to suffer my ass of. I will sacrifice my fertility for the good of humanity too."

Everyone I talked to, including my doctor, tried to assure me *it* wouldn't take long, wouldn't hurt much, and I'd be back to normal in no time, but those comforting words did little to assuage my fears and my anticipation of great suffering. They did not, after all, understand my *need* to suffer. On this conviction, I was pretty much silent, lest they think me idled or stark raving mad. The pain must be great, beyond compare, so it could stack up to all that my wife and children had endured. My youngest son, to further my case, spent a week in intensive care, barely clinging to life because an anomaly in his circulatory system caused him to be born without much blood in his body. He went into shock immediately after being born, was hooked up to every apparatus imaginable, and had multiple transfusions. Was I not destined to suffer for the suffering he endured? Let's not forget about my first son. Now there's a story. Doctors were forced to use a suction cup to get him out of the womb. As a result, he was born with a cone-shaped head that remained conical for the first eight months of his life. The sideways glances. The sniggering. The questions. The jokes. The worst was strangers trying to play horseshoes on his head. He suffered greatly.

While waiting for my operation, the month passed quickly. I feigned bravado with friends. I laughed off my fear with my enemies. On that fateful day, as I boldly trod into the doctor's office and proclaimed, "I offer myself unto you, cut away!" The doctor and his assistant were not amused. But according to operational protocol, they were jovial and tried to humor me. They distracted me with questions about my upbringing and my job. It was the old surgeon's one-two. The nurse made me answer tough questions, while the doctor stuck in the needles.

I guess they thought I wouldn't notice, but I did. I clinched my fist, lifted my head and said to the doctor, "that hurts so good. YES!" He smiled and kept slicing. He casually applied more local anesthetic, while the nurse distracted me with talk about my career as a writer

I could feel it, perhaps not in my nerve endings, but my brain registered it. I could hear it, too. It made the kind of sound a cat would make exercising its claws on a scrotum shaped scratching post, only louder. In fact, it was so loud, they could have heard it over the opening ceremonies of the 1996 Olympic games in Atlanta. He probed, cut, did a digit two-step, then he cauterized the tube.

Not only could I feel and hear it, I could smell it, too. I love to barbecue. My humble opinion is my burning scrotum smelled like the lobby of Gate Barbecue and Rib House in Kansas City. My nuts were on fire. "Oh, wow, oh wow, I am suffering the outrageous slings, slices, burning sensations and perhaps arrow shaped pin pricks in my nards."

After the doctor finished with his pyrotechnics and culinary slicing and dicing, he closed the first incision. As he completed this task, my creative brain kicked in and I conjured up an image of Santa's elves all sitting in a row sewing scrotums. I don't know, just a mental blip I guess. Then, on to number two. Ouch! I needed more anesthesia but I declined to ask. Same process. The whole time I'm grinning like hyena and talking about my career as writer. What I'm really thinking is, "is there enough pain here?" Or, should I complicate things by screaming EEEEEOOOOOWWWWWWWWW! and jumping from the table and making a dash for the door. This could—you know—augment my pain and suffering and make things interesting…something worth writing about.

As we used to say in the olden days when the disco shut down at 2 a.m., "it all ended much too soon." The stitched me up and sent me on my way with a satchel of drugs. As I left the room the doctor told me I'd be back on my feet in a matter of days, and he assured me I'd never know what happened. In his mind, the operation and the snow job were complete. My wife took me home. The drugs numbed the pain in the beginning. That made me sad. That made it seem much too easy. My oldest son was so caring, so compassionate. Whenever the phone rang and he would answer it. When the voice on the phone asked him how I was feeling, he spontaneously said, "Daddy can't come to the phone right now. His nut sack is hurting."

There would be pandemonium as we lunged for the phone and did damage control. That, my friends, was the wonderfully painful beginning.

The intense pain began the day after the procedure and lasted for four full weeks. The residual pain lasted for another two. You see the blood vessels in my tubes swelled up to the size of footballs. It felt like hemorrhoids in my scrotum. I couldn't walk straight for the entire time. I took Tylenol and hydrocodone constantly for show. But it didn't help. I spent my days on the couch with a big bag of ice in my pants. I suffered greatly, and that suffering was great cause for celebrating the pain I so disparately needed to add to my pain bank.

This was physical pain. Humiliating pain. Pain I felt ashamed to talk about in mixed company. Along with this kind of pain came minor psychological scars. I was earning the writer's pain suffrage merit badge. I endured the physical and emotional trauma of having someone fiddling around with my most sacred jewels. I met pain. I slept with it. I danced the mambo with it. I could finally walk the quiet halls of our house knowing (in my mind) that non has suffered more than I. I was a superior being with heightened perceptions.

There was no greater show if bravery. And there was enough pain to match all the pain suffered by those who fought all the wars of all worlds. I was whole and broken. I missed the draft and Vietnam, but I had a vasectomy. The triple bonus was that I didn't have to get run over by a bus, have a near-death experience, or lose any limbs. I could go forward as a writer and spew my prose everywhere. If anyone anywhere questioned my worthiness, I could answer their criticism by pulling my pants down, yanking my nut sack out and showing them the tiny scar. I could smugly say, "See here, this is why I deserve to sell a million copies of this book. Want to touch it!"

Chapter 4
Write My Son...Till You Drop

Many prolific writers were also prodigious communicators and gifted sales people. They wrote until they were—as my Anglo writer brothers and sisters would say—blue in the face. The most popular of them all then went on crusades to let the world in on the little secret that they had created a masterpiece. They talk their manuscripts up at social gatherings and on social media. They printed samples to give to friends, potential agents and publishers. The same writers who readily proclaim "I could never sell" become Og Mandino (Author of *The Greatest Salesman In the World*) reincarnates over night. They marketed, marketed, and marketed some more. They were **clever (Genius Gene #G4).** They also realized that if they created massive volumes of materials, they would not only become better writers—like musicians or expert public speakers—but something was bound fall into the right hands eventually. The clever writers know that by producing monumental volumes of work and telling EVERYBODY about it, they reduce the risk of their manuscripts ending up in a dumpster after their death. The clever writers know that the good "stuff" they get published will make all the practice/terrible stuff look better after they are famous. Publisher's are hero worshipers like everybody else, and they will take the mediocre manuscripts and edit them into blockbusters…posthumously if needed. BUT, why wait until your dead to be a hero?

    This is the terrible gamble writers take. Will our manuscripts end up in a box, perhaps chewed by rats in a cellar somewhere, or will we stumble on that piece of prose that finally breaks through the literary glass ceiling? And, will our marketing efforts pay off? Just remember, folks, that success in writing is a mathematical equation. The more you produce, the less you obsess on a single manuscript and the more fun you have. If one manuscript sucks, the other may be better. The more you produce, the more likely your friends will continue reading your manuscripts. By producing more, you increase your chance of selling something…perhaps by a factor of THOUSANDS. Finally, the more you produce, the more products you have to market. Think about the jewelry store. The store with one set of earrings will not survive. If you can produce one manuscript, you can surely produce 1000. It's simple math. Since writing is *not* real work, it should be easy, right?

    I can honestly say that I have officially attained the title of copious creator. I've written great heaping volumes of materials covering everything from the men's movement to investment property, and I'm still burping up copy and lovin' it. I've been published, published books, newspapers and magazines. I have 15 manuscripts in the works and a whole drawer full of ideas. I'm livin' the life. So, it's hard to believe that I still question whether I have paid my dues yet and whether I'm still working toward something bigger, or if my ship has sailed. So, I have resolved to keep producing and producing and loving every minute of it. Part of this is due to taking stock early and really focusing on the aforementioned writer ideologies. I asked the questions. And I actually answered them in my twenties.

How can you tell where you're *at* in your writing career? Well, it's easy. But you must start analyzing where you're at and answering questions today. If you still have the same first paragraph on a page in your typewriter that you had 30 years ago—and it's blank, you have a long ways to do. If you have 50 folders in your computer with catchy book titles—and they're all empty, stay frosty my friend and don't quit your job as chief smelter. Here are some other recommendations to help you along the way. All of these ideas are taken from a work in progress called *The World's Greatest Writer*, written many years ago by world-renowned writervational speaker Bob The Man Dino. Heed this valuable advice. Take stock and you will see "where you're at" today.

First, do a page count. If you've produced more that 10,000 pages of garbage, you're in the running for a blockbuster. Sheer stamina alone qualifies you for that blockbuster, unless, of course, you happen to be the Unibomber. But consider this: The Unibomber was published and widely distributed. His methods were, to say the least, unacceptable and deplorable, but it worked. We writer's, of course cannot employ suck tactics. It's not right. We can, however, tackle the odds of dying unpublished and habitually obscure by producing, producing, and producing some more.

It's okay to have friends read your manuscripts, even if they don't want to. But you'll need to develop a thick skin. Just tell them, "Don't run away. Here! I wrote something new. Now just read it and stop weeping." Convince yourself that what you're writing is the most brilliant work ever created. Contrary to what they say in the books for aspiring writers, the only way "real" writers can convince anyone else their writing is great, is to shove it down their throats and make them read it. All great writers do this. You should too. When all else fails, pay your friends to read your "work."

When forcing others to read your writing, however, there are some standard disclaimers and alternative approaches. Here are a few:

1. **Give your friends an out.** By forcing your friends to read your work, you're setting them up to hate you. So, when you hand off your manuscript, be sure to say, "Here's the 10,000 page

manuscript. Let me know what you think…if you have time." Do NOT box them in a corner at the next dinner party and ask, "Did you read the manuscript yet?" When they say, "No, I've been really busy," don't start screaming at them about not giving a shit about your art, etc., etc., etc. Give them time. It's been 15 years since I gave the manuscript of my first fiction novel to my friend to read. He still hasn't read it. I still love him. It's published now and selling slowly. I believe our friendship is still intact. I can confirm that when and if he ever answers the 200 emails I sent asking about his progress.

2. **Sometimes it's okay to downplay how fabulous you think the manuscript is.** When you email, snail-mail or hand someone a manuscript, let them know that it's just a draft and may be a little rough around the edges, with typos and things of that nature. You can even say, "I'm not happy with it but you may find some things you like." This puts your friends at ease and lessens their expectations. If they read it and like it, they'll let you know. Never ask them to let you know whether they like it or not. You only want them to read it for sheer enjoyment. Leave critiques up to qualified editors. If one friend tells you your manuscript sucks and you abandon it, you may be abandoning a blockbuster.

3. **I think it's ok to let friends read your manuscripts, but I firmly believe it's best NOT to let friends read your work…**unless you don't mind losing your friends. Artists and writers are pre-disposed to think their work is great. But the truth is your work may suck for some and be the cat's meow for others. Either find an editor who will read your manuscripts for free, or pay an editor to read them and give you a professional opinion. If you have a friend read your manuscript for free or for pay and they tell you, "I read your novel and it really sucks," DON'T body slam him or her to the ground and spit in his or her face and scream, "Fuck you! You don't know shit! This is the greatest fucking novel on earth! Get the fuck out of here before I pull your heart from your chest, grill it on a barbie between some chocolate like s'mores then eat it."

4. **When sharing your writing, remember that other writers are the only people who think writing is work.** Everyone else thinks writing is playing. Typing requires the least amount of energy of any kind of activity, and it's debatable whether thinking requires any energy at all. So, when you decide to let someone read your manuscript, be tactical about the wording you use during the transfer. If you're friend is a plumber, for example, say, "Here is

my manuscript. The plumber is the hero in this one. He repairs the fuck out of some pipes in chapter 6." When you deliver you manuscript to someone who actually works for a living, don't call your writing work. If it's a 300 page manuscript say, "here's something I spent two hours printing out. Boy, it took me weeks to get it printed, collated, and I punched all the sheets and put them in binders." Your friend will probably say, "Wow! That sounds like a lot of work. You did such a great job with the binding. I'll read it tonight. Thank you for the opportunity to help."

There are important psychological games all writers must play. If you're not willing to play those games, then plan to keep doing what you are currently doing; real work teaching, building, or driving, and leave the writing for those who, well, don't really want to work but want to play on the computer all day.

BONUS:
Bob The Man Dino's Sacred Scrolls For Writers - (print and place this scroll above your computer screen).

Scroll I – I will form good manuscripts by chaining myself to my chair and pretending I am my own personal writing slave. Even if I am a Negro, I will experience "White guilt" and I will alternate being master and slave; some days wielding a whip and standing over my empty chair yelling "Write NNNNiggaaaa write!" If I find this process personally offensive and visiting friends question the shackles wrapped around my chair, I will, instead, hire a dominatrix or dominator to demand that I write or lick his or her boots, thus becoming a slave to good writing habits.

Scroll II – I will greet each day with love for writing in my heart and new ideas for love scenes in my books. You know, I will think of ways to write love scenes without using terms like penis or vagina so my readers can appreciate the subtleties of romantic human interaction. I will do this knowing I may have to kill of these characters and shock my readers. I will do all of this with love in my heart.

Scroll III – I will finish the Goddamn manuscript even if it kills me. Fifty years to write a manuscript is too long. I will finish it in six months. I will stop telling people I have an idea for a book and write the damn thing. I will never say, "I wanted to be a writer." Saying that will only make me feel like a failure. As long as I draw a breath, I will persist until I succeed.

Scroll IV – I am nature's greatest writer. Finishing a manuscript is a minor miracle. I will not divide my attentions unequally between the dog, the cat, the wife, the boyfriend, the girlfriend, microbrews, the lawn, the trips to Machu Picchu, the diabetes, the benders, the gin and tonics, the job, the dog, the cat, the….EVERYTHING but writing. I will stop that! I will finish the manuscript. I will bring characters and ideas to life. I will feel like a God. The whole water-to-wine thing and parting the Red Sea will seem like child's play compared to the hero, detective wizard I have created—who I imagine is played by, say, Tom Cruse in the movie version of my book.

Scroll V – I will live this day as if it is my last. This works for me exactly as it is. When I leave my house, I will be on the look out for buses, meteors, earthquakes, zombie apocalypses, and things of that nature; anything that could unexpectedly make this my last day. As James Bond once said, "Tomorrow may never come," so I need to finish the damn manuscript today."

Scroll VI – Today I will be master of my emotions. I will hire a dominatrix or dominator to…oh, we already did that. So, here I will stare in the mirror and practice my emotions. Sadness. Gladness. Moroseness. Glibness. Joy. Fear. I am a life Shakespearean actor. The makeup I wear is my mask. I will inject all of these emotions into my characters and bring them to life, give them depth. They are not automatons, unless, of course, my book is about a dystopian future where robots rule. And I will not fly off the handle when my boss asks me to show him how I made *that* copy with the Xerox 1010 at work.

Scroll VII – I will laugh at my manuscripts and at the world (Keep perspective). Now that I have mastered my emotions, I will find joy in the fact that writing is exploring the world around me. If I can laugh at my manuscripts, I can laugh at the world. If others laugh at my manuscript, I have mastered anger, and I—in a more controlled manor—can be, as Bruce Lee once described, "like Water" and knock them across the room with my fingertips.

Scroll VIII – Today I will multiply my number of manuscripts by one. In a thousand days I will have a thousand manuscripts. Each will be worth a thousand dollars each. I will then have multiplied my value a hundred fold perhaps a thousand fold. While my friends are all talking about investing in stocks and gold, I will smile to myself. I will I have a thousand manuscripts worth, say, a billion dollars. I will find a way to share my great wealth with the world. My value in the world will be secured by selling the rights to movie director Kevin Willmott to produce a mini-series or feature film.

Scroll IX – I will act now. If I just read this, it is too late. Now was a second ago. I will try it again NOW! Ooops. Too late. Now is gone again. Let me try one more time. DAMN IT! Missed again! I will try acting tomorrow. Tomorrow I will get ahead of the game. I will do now what I cannot do a second ago. And I will do tomorrow what I did yesterday. Thus, I will have acted now and again.

Scroll X – I will pray for guidance. If that doesn't work, I will beg for guidance. If that doesn't work, I will plead to every God, entity, or plant spirit I can think of. I will schedule time to have coffee at Starbucks with those specific Gods. You know, I'll schedule some face-time for informational interviews; especially with any Zuni spirit gods, Apollo, Saraswata, Benzaiten, Al-Kutbay, Bragi, Anulap, and the African Goddess of Wisdom Seshat. Hopefully, they are not too busy fulfilling *other people's* dreams and can give a little attention to my manuscript and my life in general.

Chapter 5
Stuff Writers Need to Know

The question of what writers need to know to be great writers has come up many times at dinner parties. It's a favored discussion among the intellectually augmented and egotistically accentuated. They spend hours discussing the mind of the writer, enthusiastically debating why writers write what they write, then they form complex theories they debate over and over and over again. These crowds are particularly impressed with writers who happen to be doctors or lawyers turned writers. They, along with academics, often float the idea that in order to be a great writer you must be really smart.

I've found myself trapped in the middle of these conversations at dinner parties. It's very painful. So, the minute I hear the writer-smarter theory breach the conversation, I am compelled to strongly dissent. I climb up onto the dinner table, kick the wine glasses and plates of Seared Lesser Scaupe Duck with Red Wine and Figs aside and proclaim, "*big words and a prosperous professional career do not the great writer make! The most brilliant writers were and are, in fact, masters of the tidbit. Throughout their lives they have cultivated millions of mostly worthless morsels of information. When writing, they simply weave these dainty bits of information into a coagulated stew called prose. Granted, some happen to be doctors and lawyers. Fine. But most writers are pertinacious, scrappy, human pug dogs, both envied and disdained by most; much too opinionated and boisterous to be truly liked, but too interesting and unusual to be outwardly shunned. Writers, in fact, are most times tolerated because they tell great jokes and always have fascinating factoids at their disposal AND! people like YOU hebetudinous dolts like to swarm around writers like flies around shit because WE writers can do what most of you couldn't do if your lives depended on it…that is…tie your shoe laces straight and sling four words together to make a sentence.*"

When I am finished, I puff my chest out as far as I can, straighten my vest, dust off the shoulders of my tuxedo, then defiantly peer down at the gawking, shocked guest. Immediately, two burly waiters in tails and top hats drag me off the table and kick me to the curb. Days later I'm served with a lawsuit to recover damages for the broken Chateau Baccarat stemware, Royal Copenhagen Flora Danica 5 Serrated Edge tableware and wasted food that was personally prepared by Chef Ramsey who stormed around the house dropping F-bombs after my unsolicited soliloquy. I shrug it off, toss the summons in the trash and say to myself, "it was terribly snobbish of them to not applause after my masterful delivery."

I stand firm in my assertions. The true masters of the morsel have an anecdote for everything and a story related to a story. The best writers have been accused of suffering from "grandpa syndrome." They begin every story with, *I remember when…I read somewhere that…* or

Did I tell you about the time... or *When I was your age...* or, the best one of them is *I met (name your celebrity) once back in..."*

The aforementioned habit, for them, often began at age five. This caused alarm in many parents, who, unfortunately, resorted to popular therapies for their children, such as, Ritalin and other methamphetamines. The most insightful parents of them all, of course, recognize the true genius of their children and instead of discouraging the little tykes, engaged them, encouraged them, THEN gave them Ritalin.

The bottom line is as follows: If you are going be a great writer, you must begin cultivating tidbits today. Make the investment and expand your actuarial tidbit table. What kinds of tidbits would be the most useful? I'm glad you asked. Let's segue into the real meat of this chapter. Here are the top 10 types of tidbits to accrue for those who want to be truly great writers and revered at dinner parties:

1) **Know interesting facts about all sorts of writers**, especially the obscure Armenian-Russian novelists of the 1700s and 1800s. Also include a good mix of Chinua Achebe, Mary Jo Putney, Jerzy Kosinski, James Baldwin and Sero Hanzadyan. I aced great American literature by only reading cliff notes. Drinking beer with my friends in Aggieville was way more interesting than reading *My Antonia*. Props to Willa, but I was a young Negro in Kansas. I wanted to get out Kansas, not study Midwesterner culture. I felt equally as strongly about Mark Twain (more in book #2). The idea here is not to spend too much time trying to figure out why writers wrote what they wrote, but learn what they drank or smoked while they were writing. Most of the great Kansas writers like William Allen White probably spent a fair amount of time in the bar as well. You see, process is two thirds of the process of writing. The most interesting of writers were the ones who had favorite drinking places, led bawdy and ruckus lives, were defiant and antisocial, broke all the rules and led lives that were nothing short of scandalous. Lots of tidbits there. Soak them up, as many as you can, then spew them forth in your writings and in idle conversations without apology.

2) **Know the origins of words.** Few know—nor do many care—about the origins of words, but words hold the answers to the meaning of life in general. If you know the origins of words, you know more than everyone else does…by default. For example, did you know that the word berserk means "bear shirt?" Norse mythology described a famous, furious fighter who refused to

wear armor in battle. Instead, he preferred to wear a fashionable bearskin fastened to one shoulder during marauding excursions and tribal skirmishes. This Viking lunatic was considered a hero and a character that inspired a major fashion statement and an awesome word. Let's keep going. Did you know that a diaper wasn't always a breechcloth for babies? NO! Its original purpose was use as a tablecloth. It was so absorbent, however, its default use was for baby diapers. Eventually, that became its primary use. Tablecloths thereafter were bought from Pier 1 and were generally made from synthetic materials—not quite as soft on baby privates.

3) **All writers should have one copy of *Writer's Market*** and be familiar with who's publishing what. This could, I'm sad to say, be some of the most useless information you could posses, but it's nice to have one in case another writer mentions it. The only section in this book that's truly useful these days is the section about self-publishing with Amazon (gratuitous endorsement). The world of publishing has changed immensely, and it's important to know how to do it your self. I'll let you in on a secret. There's nothing like smugly saying (at a fancy dinner party), "I publish my own books and sell shit-loads of them on the Internet and other places too." The reveal is, of course, that you posses a rare knowledge. Many frustrated writers have self-published their own books. Many of those books are collecting mold in basements all over New England. The cleverest of writers have figured out how to actually sell books. Once you posses this knowledge, people will try to pick your brain like a condor on a carcass. Dance around them like Muhammad Ali. If you give away too much of this knowledge, they will have no further use for you, and they may even fear you. You will cease to be an amusing writer and become a formidable force to be reckoned with. People will tag you as superior, knowledgeable and profitable. You will be branded a publisher. By revealing too many publishing secrets you risk being shunned or feared by those who are not your equal.

4) **Know current events.** Not so much, though, that the knowledge becomes unwieldy. You don't want any single piece of information to dominate the rest. You *do* want additional information on some of the more complex issues of the day. A few statistics might help too. Statistics can make you sound smart. When discussing an important political issue, you can seamlessly announce, "a recent Joe Smederman pole suggest that 52 percent of all people in Gainesville, Florida, support Usain Bolt for president of the United States." Intermittent statistics are like

electricity in conversations and writing. Politicians love them. Statistics open minds to questions. Questions generate attention. Attention can get you a book deal or elected. Learn to love statistics.

5) **Read reference books.** They contain the juiciest kind of tidbits that make even doctors and lawyers say, "whoa! You're smart!" There's a wealth of reference manuals to choose from. There are environmental almanacs, dictionaries of famous composers, and even some obscure reference materials such as *Folk Medicine: Cures and Curiosities*, by Edward F. Dolan—which I happen to have in my collection. To show you how fascinating these materials are, here's a little tidbit from *Folk Medicine*: "The headache is, in part, responsible for one of the world's earliest surgeries; trepanning, or trephining. The surgery, which is still performed today, involves boring into and removing sections of the skull. It dates back some 25,000 years to the Stone Age, and is thought to have been employed to free the patient of the demons of headache or insanity." This is a procedure I sometimes think would be useful for some berserk members of our society. Fascinating, right? Let me tell you, tidbits don't get much more riveting!

6) **Watch TV newsmagazines.** I know, I know, you only watch PBS. Get over that. Television is one of the best sources of nonessential, beguiling nonsensical information. *Dateline*, as you know, tops the chart, especially the trivia question and name-that-tune segment. There are current episodes available, but you can also find back-episodes on Youtube. I love Ann Curry, Stone Phillips, Jane Pauley and Lester Holt. These are just a few of the great journalists involved in the show. There are many other engaging personalities involved in this show and they all believe in their work. I can tell. Don't make the social faux pas, however, of citing your television sources when exercising your tidbit adroitness. Where TV tidbits come from is irrelevant. If you say, "Hoda Kotb said on *Dateline* last night..." you're conceding that you might be into TV tidbit glorification. Spit out the factoid as if it were your own. There is no such thing as factoid plagiarism unless you proclaim, "My TV documentary on teen murderers concluded..." Oh, and please don't watch cable TV. That will only confuse you. You won't be able to stop clicking the remote with your thumb, even while you're sleeping. Too much information is like a rich blend of gasoline and alcohol, and—like a funny car—you'll burn out your mental pistons in a matter of months. So, the TV short list consists of *CNN* (especially the

Albino Anderson Cooper), *Rachel Maddow, 48 Hours, 60 Minutes, Norman Goldman Podcasts,* and reruns of *Oprah.* **(Genius Gene #G5: Oprah)** Nothing else will do. All other news is paid for and fake. If you quote any current or former daytime talk show hosts other than Oprah Winfrey, you'll be socially shunned. Dinner party invitations will be revoked, people will suddenly forget who you are, and time will stop. Life, as you know it will end, and you will die alone and broke in a fleabag hotel. Keep in mind that even conservatives love liberals who can toss the conversation salad…so to speak. Everybody knows it's really boring for everybody to be agreeable all the time.

7) **Social media is a bit of a pickle these days.** Even though I started this book in 1996, I saw social media coming. While publishing my community newspapers and my self defense magazine, I had two pagers, one cell phone, a micro-cassette tape recorder and pepper spray all snug in my faux police tactical utility jacket. The bullet slots were empty, of course. The coolest tools I carried were the two pagers I leased. They were pagers that could deliver daily newscasts and weather casts. I got my news delivered via satellite before everyone else. While staring into these tiny green screens churning out headline stories, I saw the future of mobile communications. Today there's smart phones, *Twitter, Youtube, Facebook, SnapChat,* and a million other news sources. Ignore them all, especially the comment sections. Media folks will be happy to hear this. I say stick with my recommendations in #6, but supplement that information by using *Wiki, IMDB, Youtube* documentaries and *NPR.* Keep your information flow organized, constant and tempered. Otherwise there's a shitstorm of information out there that will only overwhelm and confuse you. You don't want that confusion to sink into your writing or conversations. People have an uncanny sense for sniffing out information that's, well, how should I say this…information that's STUPID. Tidbits can be powerful and can inspire conversation and stories. Stupid information only stunts our intellectual growth.

8) **For entertainment tidbits,** DON'T—I repeat—DON'T rely on gossip television exclusively, especially *TMZ.* Secretly rifle through copies of the *National Enquirer,* the *Star,* and *People Magazine* while waiting to pay for your groceries at the market. Do it quickly and surreptitiously. If any of your intellectually acute associates catches you with a *Star* in hand, you'll be spurned, rebuffed, a social pariah; and it's not a pretty sight. You'll have to publicly wear a scarlet "TT" for *tainted tidbit.* Surf the Internet once a week for

current tidbits. While surfing, click on one of those links that, for example, advertises the *Top 50 Stars Who Are Now Working at Wal-Mart*. Try to make it through all 50. That's good stuff. But do NOT—and I repeat—DO NOT click on the link that advertises the *Top 10 Photos of Animals Eating Babies While Helpless Crowds Watch*. You'll be sorry. You can't really walk that stuff back in your head or talk about it with friends. That's like trying to describe all the best *Failed Youtube* videos you've ever watched. Useless information only gets trapped in your head and crowds out the useful information. Rather than try to describe useless videos to others, do them a favor and slip them a sleeping pill instead. The result will be the same. Make it a habit to strategically view or watch info you can easily regurgitate. If you want to have a little more fun with this process, watch *Drunk History* Youtube episodes. That's something to talk about.

9) **For general news tidbits, read the four times;** *New York Sunday Times*, *Los Angeles Sunday Times*, *The London Times*, and digital *Time Magazine* (which is owned by the same people who publish *People Magazine*). You can also read *USA Today* without fear of condemnation. When *USA Today* first debuted, most mediocrity-fearing journalist and intellectual wannabes loathed it's appearance and deemed it the McDonald's of newspapers. Over the years, however, it has proved itself to be a top-notch mediocre newspaper, full of quality superficial writing and all the bells and whistles people love. Talk show hosts, local journalist, and everyone else (even PR hacks), rely on all of the aforementioned newspapers for tasty tidbits and story ideas.

10) **The Internet**, as I mentioned, is firmly established as a valuable resource for massive amounts of information. As I have also mentioned, too much information on too many things is socially and intellectually detrimental. Overload can cause a Soviet Union-like reaction. Your brain will revolt and splinter itself. Your memory banks will succeed from one another and you'll take to drinking, drugs and lewd and lascivious activities until you die alone and forgotten in a seamy transient hotel in San Francisco's Tenderloin. To prevent that from happening, I recommend you heed my advice and go back to the basics. Go to the local library and read as many illustrated informational children's books as you can find. I recommend the *Dorling Kindersley* series of *Eyewitness* children's books and Stephen Biesty's series of *Incredible Cross-sections* books. These are great picture books that won't cause your brain to short circuit and explode. These books are great ballast

for tsunami-like information flow of the Internet. Don't get sucked into researching for general information on the Internet. There's so much information there that you could grow quite old before you zero in on what you're looking for or anything tangible. Plus, you'll inevitably get suckered into clicking on a link that promotes *Child Stars...What They Look Like Today* and that will lead to clicking on other useless information links. Fifteen hours later you'll give up and start watching Youtube *Failed* videos again. If using the Internet for research, find the fastest computer known to man, and search only for specific subjects. Don't forget that the best computer in the world is still balanced (barely in some cases) squarely on your shoulders, and the *best* resource is still your local library (those that survived the Internet explosion.).

11) **See lots of movies.** All movies reflect some reality and feed the imagination. Movies are cultural and intellectual sounding boards and excellent educational resources. Whenever discussing movies, NEVER give away the plot. EVER! If you give away the plot once, you'll be tempted to do it again and again. This is called "spoiler superiority." You'll convince yourself you're doing others a favor by divulging the plot, especially if you did *not* enjoy the movie. What you're actually doing is exposing your UN-cleverness. People will hate you for spoiling their opportunity to learn for themselves. If you suffer from spoiler superiority, there is still hope for you. Watch back episodes of *Siskel & Ebert*. Become masterful at analyzing movies without giving away the show. This skill will ultimately translate into your prose and conversation as well. *Siskel & Ebert* set the bar for clever social conversational exchange. They were the masters of the tidbit and they knew it. You can't know everything about everything but you CAN know a little about a lot of things.

12) **Read lots of books too**! But keep in mind that books are *not* ideal tidbit sources. It takes too long to find juicy tidbits in a novel. They're great fun to read, but best to discuss in a book group setting. Talking too much about a book the person you're talking to has *not* read is the equivalent of boring that person to tears. Don't do that. If you do that, you obviate the need to read said book. In which case, you're doing society and the literary market a great disservice. Keep in mind, too, that *you* may be excited about authors other people may not care about. Don't exclude all other authors to serve your one *master* author. If someone has not read any books by your master author, do not shun them. One writer's master author is another's suck-ass loser author. Like *Siskel &*

Ebert you must be willing to discuss the merits of any author—even one you know nothing about—by asking great questions. The ability to ask great questions is the real art form here, not your ability to bloviate about one book or your favorite author or authors. Reading different books by different authors gives us the foundation for formulating great questions.

Do all these things and you will be whole, fulfilled, and you will have achieved what most non-writers only dream of. You will be tidbit endowed, and you will know what only truly great writers *need* to know.

Chapter 6
Everybody's a Writer for Crissakes

Whenever I think of writing and writers, I think of that old comedy bit where someone is having a heart attack in a comedy club. Seeing the person is in distress, a good citizen stands up and yells, "Is there a doctor in the house!" Immediately, fifteen writers step forward and hand the dying man a copy of their manuscripts, treatments, or samples of their blog posts. This leads me, unceremoniously, head-on into my next outrageous assertion: EVERYBODY IS A WRITER THESE DAYS!

That's particularly true in our new hyper-electronic centered communications society. Even programmers today are "authors." Some once used popular visual-based programming software called *Authorware*. The advent of the personal computer put writing within reach of just about every wannabe writer in the land with a pre-baked, fully baked or half-baked idea. Some even felt that if they could pound out a couple of sentences, format it into a web page, pull some clip art and post it, they were suddenly published celebrity writers, authors, or investigative journalists. It has become increasingly harder to identify the *real* writers among fake ones; almost as hard as it is to identify the real Martians among us. Believe me, I've tried.

This presents a variety of problems for the legitimate writers and journalist with real degrees from accredited English and Journalism departments worldwide. A writer with a related degree has quickly become an Albatross in the world of modern writing. It is a sad unforeseeable truth that comes at a time when writers—journalist in particular—almost reached a point where writing was considered more of a profession rather than a past time.

Reporters, in particular, are the coolest writers of them all. They learned to craft brilliant stories on the fly, sometimes even expertly dictating stories to editors over the phone while out in the field. The very best reporters could produce newspaper gold, so to speak, and they helped make many publishers very wealthy. Reporters were also willing to put their freedom and their lives on the line to protect society, their sources, and their trade. Sadly, that kind of reporter is quickly on the decline along with newspapers and magazines. As print publications disappear, so do the finances to defend and protect reporters from lawsuits and even death. This makes investigative journalism an even more risky endeavor for inexperienced journalist.

News today is instant, often driven by the quest for clicks Overnight web sensations don't pay as much attention to detail. They're driven by a hunger for clicks and instant celebrity. Cyberspace wannabe fake writers *are* wreaking havoc on the profession, devaluing the trade *and* creating "fake" news. Trump has a point. Fake reporters are diluting the media pool. They are un-credentialed and undisciplined and they have immediate access to publishing. They deligitimizie the "real" news and, unfortunately, there's not a damn thing we can do about it. Sadly, I believe the journalism degree won't be worth the paper it's printed on unless there is a required advanced certification and required continuing education. You know, like LCSWs or psychologist; important people like that.

This problem impacts all workplaces as well, especially at marketing and advertising agencies. I've had some personal experience with this. In 1996 I worked as a senior writer for Creative Media Development, one of the largest marketing and communications firms in Portland, Oregon.

Project planning meetings took place seemingly every three to five minutes. There were proposal meetings, project meetings, pre-meeting meetings, meeting planning meetings and even post-mortem project meetings. One day, I was in a post-project-acceptance-content-planning-and-production meeting. Included in the meeting was one writer (me), producer, account executive, designer, and department manager. At one point, the department manager scanned the room and asked, "So, we've got this project locked in with the client but everybody has a full billable schedule. We have a budget for writing, but I'm not sure who's actually going to write the content for this Intel DSR 5000 Router Training?" Before I had a chance to speak, every individual in the room alternately proclaimed that they would write the content. And there you have it. The only degreed, professional writer in the room was me, but everyone *believed* they were writers.

None of my associates ever said to me, "Raymond, you're the degreed, trained writer here. You and only you should write copy for this project. You'll deliver the best value for our client's dollars."

I'm not sure anyone cared that I was real writer with a real journalism and mass communications degree. The assumption was that the client was paying extremely well, so getting the project done was paramount, and it didn't matter who wrote the copy as long as it got written and came in under budget. To achieve that goal—in some cases—interns were hired to write the copy and the principle writer went into meetings to defend the copy written by the intern. If the client hated the copy, the intern was fired. If the client loved the copy, the representing writer or creative director bowed and received the bouquet. By the time all was said and written, the client paid the bill and EVERYBODY WAS STILL A WRITER at the end of the day. The intern—who had a degree in wildlife biology—was hired as senior staff writer and the agency wheel kept turning and turning and turning and never looking back.

Maybe no one in his or her right mind should ever *really* want to be a writer—especially for a marketing agency, and especially after reading this book. Writing, in general, is a sometimes-lonely trade, wrought with uncertainty. What you create is subject to great scrutiny and criticism by clients, the public, by friends and by self. Even the worst of writers thinks they know great writing. To be a really good writer requires years and years of practice and experience, and years of experience are still not enough to guarantee a high paying job or publishing contract. Sure, there are a few prodigies and talented people out there, but many of them end up as one-hit-wonders or in PR firms getting paid ridiculous amounts of money to write pure dreck.

A sustainable writing career requires stamina and a lot of hard knocks. What typically happens with writing hacks is when the writing is good, they love the praise, but when it's bad, they default to the fact that their real job is accounting, or video production, or sweeping the floors. Nothing is more uncomfortable than being in a conference call with a client that out of the blue announces, "This content really sucks. Who wrote this crap?" There's almost always sudden plausible deniability and—wait for it—no writers in the room.

The real writer, on the other hand, must be accountable, whether the writing is good or bad, and at times they must be willing to sometimes defend their choices fervently to a dispassionate editor or client. That means describing and defending the thought processes, grammatical styling, voice decisions, and even some minutely intricate intellectual considerations related to the overall tone and audience. Hacks are usually not willing to dig that deep. They'll usually sit and take it and call the client an asshole when the client hangs up the line. They'll never acknowledge mediocrity, and many will find a new profession or get promoted to creative director if they play the game right.

Writers today are faced with the same classic dilemma that the designers of the 80s faced. When the Macintosh entered the market, millions of half-artist and first-year art students entered the marketplace and began clamoring for design work. Hence, the designers who spent 20 years perfecting their trade suddenly had to compete with Biff from Santa Barbara who had a Macintosh, surf board, a nose earring, and a couple of projects done pro bono during art school in their portfolio. Biff would also work for minimum wage.

In those days, designers with 20-plus years of experience would normally charge $80 an hour. After quoting their hourly rate, they dreaded hearing the inevitable phrase, "That's' really expensive. I can get it done for half that." My experienced designer friends in San Francisco used to fume about this development over Martini's at John's Grill. Finally, they reluctantly gave in and got Macintoshes and began going head-to-head with said neophytes.

Ironically, 20 years later, the same companies that took chances on those first year art students and LOST money on time wasted and lost clients, returned to the seasoned designers who could design *and* articulate the ideas behind their ideas. Most people who started out as Mac designers are no longer designing anything. Those neophyte designers are now designing web sites and blogging or went into marketing for a start-up or are working at an insurance firm. You see, it's one thing to create beautiful graphics and design, but it takes years of experience and professional interaction and sophistication to accumulate the vocabulary to explain it. Thus, being articulate is essential for design and writing.

Such is what's happening in the writing field. The real writers who could spin words into gold on any subject imaginable were bypassed for the effervescent college grad with no experience. While bubbly and eager, those college grads had little depth from which to draw on, few resources beyond sheer willingness, and in the demanding world of writing, that was just not enough.

Companies that allowed employees in the company to write on anything, no matter what their real job was, now realize that doing so was a mistake. The misses mounted more than the hits, and they realize that with a real, focused writer, they could have award-winning writing more times than not. That kind of writing, however, cost money. And those kinds of writers were an odd bunch, like me.

Most people have the ability to write exceptionally well. But that, I contend, does not a professional writer make. The professional writer, like any Olympian, writes by day, and if he or she has any strength left, writes into the wee hours of the night, typically by candlelight.

I cringe when I see a job post that asks for samples of blog posts. I have NO blog posts in my portfolio. I may never have any. But, I have written thousands of leads. After all, isn't a blog just a glorified lead? Those of you who know what a lead is will answer *yes*. Those of you who don't should run to the nearest community college and take an *Intro to Journalism* class. With a little more history of journalism, you'll have the potential to be a highly effective *real* professional writer.

Chapter 7
Academic Study: Writer VS Kids

Kids are the natural born predator of the writer. Before I continue with this story, however—and perhaps say some things my children might one-day hate me for—I must proclaim that I unequivocally love my children very much. I am, however, convinced that the objectives of the human child are in complete conflict with the objectives of the adult writer.

Let me elaborate. There seems, in fact, to be an inherent predacious relationship that exist between the writer and the child that has evolved over many centuries. Children, I believe, are genetically predisposed to deliberately thwart the efforts of professional writers and prevent them from doing ANY writing at ANY time. This relationship is no secret to anyone who has ever attempted to write anything coherent while there is a child within 10 feet. Children, like Basset hounds, have an uncanny ability to sniff out both writers and fear. Many anthropological and historical records confirm that the child is a relentless, unforgiving tormentor of the writer.

Some 19th and 20th century thinker-writers have been quite clear on this subject, having suffered their own humiliation at the hands of children. Their observations and intellectual musings prove that this relationship is not a figment of their imagination, but a well-documented social phenomenon.

Julius Huxtable, a noted controversial writer on evolution during the late 1800s, made this observation in his essay, *"Evolution of the Species and Writers Too"*:

"...under these circumstances, to deny that the characteristics of animals, plants, and writers were created by divine intervention, severely limits the scope of a grander hypothesis. The scientific aspects are conclusive and may be passed without further notice that the writer was implanted on Earth in the original form of a chicken and passed through the essential stage to a fish-like creature to a land vertebrate, and eventually back to, in theory, an upright invertebrate called a homo-writer-erectus."

Those same really smart people found that as the writer evolved, important archeological discoveries showed evidence of the antagonistic relationship between adult writers and juvenile Homo sapiens. This related excerpt is from Elliot Bradley's book *"Anti-Writer Tendencies of Juvenile Homo sapiens"*:

"The theory of natural selection suggest that the child threatened the survival of the adult writer by taunting, teasing, belittling, and even openly humiliating the adult writer in common areas of ancient village sites. Archeological evidence showed that to retaliate, the adult writer often gave chase to juveniles, captured them and gave them

early style "noogies." This is evidenced by a worn away area of the skulls of juveniles that could have been made by a bare knuckle. Other digs unearthed hieroglyphics and pottery paintings of children burning writing implements, painting stick figures over manuscripts, and one dig even indicated that multiple adult Homo sapiens, out of shear frustration, lodged what looked like a number two pencil into the skull of a young juvenile."

Cultural anthropologists have extensive proof that the child, seeking revenge for years of abuse, advocated making slaves of all writers, and openly articulated this position. These excerpts from Ben Styver's book, "*Writer: Slave or Parent*," documented the sentiments of many children:

"It may be safely said, based on my observations, that the child openly asserts its superiority over the writer, but because the writer has proliferated in such numbers, the greatest obstacle to the abolition of the writer cannot be accomplished easily. One child is quoted as saying, 'There is an insuperable bar to an amalgamation of writers and children, so if we cannot rid ourselves of this evil, we should make slaves of them, lest we have the misfortune of watching them multiply 10-fold in the course of one century.'"

Eric Frommier, the exalted French psychologist wrote extensive dissertations on the conflicts that exist between the modern 20th century writer and the child. His most popular work is *Child vs. Writer, Writer vs. Child, Writer vs. Himself*. Frommier writes:

"In the course of normal development, any pleasures the writer may experience undergoes a radical modification when his external world is invaded by the child. The pleasure-principle so noted by Sigmund Freud, is hence replaced by the 'reality of pain principle,' whereby the writer's mental apparatus learns to postpone the pleasure and satisfaction of writing to tolerate prolonged feelings of pain caused by the antics of the child."

There is also evidence of this conflict in the writing of Shakespeare, Poe, and Hemingway. It is said that Hemmingway led a tortured life merely because children existed. The antagonists in many great works of literature are said to be, in some cases, metaphors for toddlers. Scottish writer Inis McGreely wrote one of the most famous literary works on writers and children in 1768. McGreely aptly titled his dissertation '*Hell.*' This excerpt reflects his theory that children *are* a divine punishment for all writers:

"Some have said that hell is a place of divine punishment after death; a place located at the center of the earth where, should you be so unfortunate to inhabit this place, you will experience seven degrees of pain. It is a place for the wicked, the wretched, the scum, and, unfortunately, for writers who cannot endure the torments of children. In hell there are seven gates named Holly, Justin, Megan, Amy, Nicole, Brian, and Anthony. The writer must choose one. Behind each gate is a different torment. Behind Megan, for example, is a 4-year-old who throws a perpetual tantrum in a crowded shopping mall. She will throw herself to the ground, scream at the top of her lungs, spit fire, kick, and call you names. You will spend eternity trying to calm her down. So, not only must the writer endure the burning fires of hell, but he or she must also endure other hell torments which are disproportional to any crimes which may have been committed in life."

Legendary filmmaker Stephen Speilberger was particularly fascinated with the subject of writers and kids. His goal was to explore this relationship in a movie called "*Ohio Joe in the Den of Doom*," a story about a writer in a suburban neighborhood who must pass through a perilous gauntlet of kids to get to his computer in the den and write one full page of text. We acquired the original script treatment. In this scene, Ohio Joe attempts to write a short story but is confronted by Junior, his 5-year-old son.

Junior: "Dad I want to play on the computer."
Ohio: "Son, do you see me using the computer? What do you think I'm doing here?"
Junior: "Nothing."
Ohio: "Do you think what I am doing is important?"
Junior: "No! My stuff is more important."

INTERACTION: Dad laughs because he can't believe what his son is saying. Son sticks out his tongue and sprays spittle all over dad's face. Dad loses train of thought. Writing effort is effectively destroyed.
MUSIC: Segue in music, something along the lines of *Raiders of the Lost Arc* style.

SCENE: Ohio spends the night huddled next to his computer, wearing only bikini underwear and a scanty shirt, listening for sounds of kids stirring. At dawn he slowly works his way into his chair and begins to write another story. He thinks he's home free. He thinks he's alone. Only minutes after he begins, he is startled to find Biff, his youngest son peering up at him from behind the computer, hissing and drooling like, um, that creature in *Aliens*.

Biff: "Dad, there's some buttons behind your computer."
Ohio: "I know, son, don't press any of those. Step away from the computer. NOW!"
Biff: "Why dad?"
Ohio: "If you press any buttons, your brain will be sucked right out of your head."
Biff: "Na-ah."
Ohio: "Don't press any of those buttons son! Don't do It? Step away from the machine?"

INTERACTION: Son presses button. Computer explodes. Dad has no time to save the document. Story is destroyed. Dad gives chase to son who finds sanctuary with mom in the kitchen. Dad discovers mom suspended from the ceiling by tons of crystallized, gummy maple syrup strands. She has a dozen eggs in her hand and is getting ready to make breakfast. Dad grabs a spatula and threatens to crack the eggs. Mom turns to her children and hisses. They back off. Dad cracks the eggs anyway and runs. The kids and mom give chase to dad.

SFX: Wind tunnel type sound effects, ground level steady cam chase scene. Have mom secretly clinging to the undercarriage of the Bronco as dad makes his escape with Newton, their dog. Newton, by the way, has been impregnated. Later show the dog explode and have a toothy, screaming, smart-mouthed kid leap out of his stomach and run away.

Oh, by the way, dad has been impregnated too. Later have him give birth to a boogger-covered, snot-nosed little rug rat. Oh, Oh, Oh, and get this, every writer on earth has been impregnated. Show kids exploding from their stomachs all over the place, pounding on keyboards, climbing on the heads of writers while they try to write, talking real loud for no reason, trying to pick their little brothers up by the tongue with a pliers, and some even drooling on manuscripts, then eating them once they're softened.

#END SCRIPT

These are just a few examples of the textured and tempestuous relationships that exist between writers and children. The only writers who have not suffered as much from the antics of the child is the children's book author. Their relationship, however, is tenuous at best. The children's book author still harbors much disdain for children that is the byproduct of deep-rooted resentment for centuries of abuse and misunderstandings.

It seems the children's book author was once—and is still today—considered by kids to be a mystical, magical, lucky charm of sorts. The child's natural instinct is to *not* thwart the efforts of this type of writer, but, instead, to capture it and rub its belly. If a child can capture and rub the soft underbelly of the children's book author, not only will the author create stories of amusement and adventure, but the author will bring that child great luck and perhaps conjure up heaping truckloads of chocolate bars.

Consequently, evidence of this phenomenon can be found in long-abandoned, ancient village shopping mall dig sites in western Kansas. Modern evidence of this is still seen in shopping malls worldwide. It's not unusual, for example, to see a children's book author flat on his back in a JC Penny store with a gang of giggling moppets huddled around him rubbing his stomach and wishing for something ridiculous like a seven foot Black Panther super hero doll while chanting, "We don't want no omnibus, just write something clever for us."

Chapter 8
IT'S CHIC TO BE VAGUE:
Or Some, Sommer, Sommest.

As a professional writer, I've had the opportunity to spend great amounts of time with other professional writers, editors and publishers. I've always marveled at their conversational skills, particularly their ability to babble on about any old thing, and their skills at keeping audiences in suspense *(Genius Gene #G6 – Gift of Improvisation)*. They also have an uncanny ability to enthusiastically debate worldly topics such as the advantage of using contractions in writing.

Around 1986, during a particularly blue period of my life, my ears, for a time, grew much larger than they are now, and I began listening more closely to what people were saying. All of my senses were elevated by my permutations. I could hear more. I could process more. Eventually—and this is a shocking part—it dawned on me that the people I thought were really smart—weren't really smart at all. This was a devastating revelation for a young writer, so full of optimism and hope for the human race; and a young writer seeking truth in my fellow humans.

I discovered that the banter of some of my intellectual counterparts was based purely on, well, hot air. I also discovered that there exists among these individuals an unwritten understanding that requires the regularly practice of truly banal, vaporous banter, which also involves extended conversations that evolves around vacuous assumptions. Their resolve goes beyond normal conversation and the natural use of tidbits, and is much more deliberate and insidious.

During these conversations, many statements are unsubstantiated figments of the imagination, made with the sole intent of prolonging some hackneyed discourse with some unsuspecting neophyte. Pontification is a standard modus operandi, but any rigorous vetting of these postulations would show that they fail to hold water. *And*, when too many questions arise about the major points of contention, the discussion is rudely and unceremoniously changed or terminated.

I found many of my counterpart editors, writers, and publishers particularly guilty of these practices because many of these privileged individuals believe it is their duty to be nothing less than scintillating ALL the time. They believe they are the natural heir apparent to the intellectual conversation throne. The last thing on earth my comrades ever want to do is appear "simple." They believe "culture" was created by, for, and as a tribute to their vast intellect. In contrast, I'm a simple Jamaican-American lad from the country.

During this four-year "blue" period, I studied these individuals, took copious notes on their social patterns, and even infiltrated their little secret clubs of braggarts, egomaniacal pseudo intellectuals, pompous phonies and generally boring people who will willingly fritter away your valuable time without regret if you allow them to.

I submit, herewith, my findings. I must, however, warn you that upon reading these notes, you may never look at another writer, editor, or publisher the same way again. Be forewarned, too, that if an individual with these tendencies ever gets "wise" to the fact that you are "on" to them, the conversation may turn apoplectic. So, if you find yourself in a position where you must exit a particularly dull conversation or confront one of my kind, always keep a weapon handy; a dictionary, thesaurus, miniature encyclopedia, a bat or, in some extreme cases, ask Siri on your smart phone.

These are the traits and patterns I observed:

- **They Practice Conversatium Nebulus** - Only discuss things that are vague and open for wide interpretation.
- **Most of the time** they start a pompous declaration with the word "most."
- **When they manufacture statistics, 90 percent of the time they rely on manufactured statistics**. The most common statistic references include 90 percent, 50 percent, and 30 percent. These are tells, as they say in poker. They use 90 percent when they want to look informed and be *right* absolutely. They use 50 percent to assure that they have a 50 percent chance of being right or wrong, therefore deflecting any suspicions about their dubious assertions. They use 30 percent when you don't know squat about what they're talking about and they know they are probably wrong.
- **If you ever question** the validity of their facts, they say, "That's ridiculous" and walk away.
- **If backed into a corner** and pressed for proof of theory, they will say, "Barkeep, another vodka tonic for my friend here" even if you're at an AA meeting.
- **If confronted with difficult questions**, they will ignore you and keep talking. What they have to say is far too important AND for your own good.
- **They talk as if they're lecturing to a group of freshman**, and only allow for a two-minute question and answer session. When the time is up they'll abruptly shout, "CLASS DISMISSED!"

- **If they think they're boring someone to tears**, they keep talking anyway. It's not a conversation. What they have to say is terribly important AND for your own good.
- **They talk excessively about food and restaurants**, food and restaurants, food and restaurants. These topics are great intellectual smoke screens. The really cool people only talk about restaurants for about five minutes than move on to world politics. Listen carefully to the restaurant braggarts and bullies. They'll keep talking about restaurants, especially the expensive ones but never mention how they wept like a baby when the bill came, made a scene with the general manager, and had to be dragged out of the restaurant…all the while screaming, "It was so tiny! How could it cost that much!"
- **They learn everything they can about one opera**, one Broadway play, one jazz musician, one slacker band, one Shakespearean play; basically one of everything and they tell the same stories about the same things over and over and over and never remember that they told the same store over and over and over and over and over…

Time is precious people. If, while talking to these kinds of people, you suddenly become aware that there is a loud ticking sound in our ears, you must realize that it's not a bomb. That, my friends, is the minutes of your life ticking away while someone else is using you for their own intellectual gratification. If you don't stand up for your rights and assert yourself, minutes can turn into hours. Hours can turn into days, and days can turn into years. You'll be old and gray, languishing in a nursing home in Sequim, Washington, reflecting back on the countless hours of your life wasted by others. Those millions of hours could have been spent getting an advanced degree or inventing something or, or writing something, or having sex or something. Instead, all you have to show for your life is…well, wasted time. Don't make the same mistakes I made. Do something. Be somebody. You can still make a difference. DO IT NOW! GET OUT OF THAT CONVERSATION NOW!

Chapter 9
The Writer's Habitat

The apartment is the most important status symbol of the creative underclass, particularly in larger cities, such as New York and San Francisco. Amongst the creatively endowed, the apartment provides a common denominator; a plebian factor to which writers can relate. And, the apartment is a perennial topic of discussion amongst the coffee klatches, nightclubs, and vintage shops that writer's frequent.

The apartment also—unfortunately—provides a great means of escaping assimilation and homeownership. For many writers, the apartment as a crutch and provides an excuse to do such obscene things as cut great works of art from the pages of *Smithsonian Magazine*, put them in expensive frames, hang them on the walls and pretend they're originals. Here are some other things I have observed about the writer's habitat and another handful of brilliant assumptions.

FUEL FOR SCINTILLATING DEBATES

Amongst writers, the apartment provides fodder for spirited discussions. Who has great views? How many rooms are there? Roommate horror stories. Writers have even been known to brazenly compare their security deposits in public places too.

FEAR OF BEING ALONE

A certain social dualism exists for the writer because his natural preference is to be alone. Being alone, however, presents few opportunities to share his ideas, which he feels are vital to the survival of the species. Roommates provide a situation of forced human interaction. This satisfies the writer, but can be somewhat burdensome for a roommate, unless that roommate happens to be another writer. In the end, though, the scales are somewhat balanced. All roommates have someone to feed on their particular neurosis.

INTERIOR AGORAPHOBIA

The studio apartment—which is a big den with a kitchen and bathroom in the same room—provides the perfect habitat for the writer, because no matter how far he paces, he's always within arms reach of his writing machine (like an abdominizer, but doesn't come with whips and chains). After a night of turbid espresso sipping and raucous chess playing at Caffe Riggio, the writer, upon awakening in the morning, has approximately 30 seconds to use the bathroom, make coffee and be ready to write. If it takes more than 30 seconds, the writer will throw up his hands in frustration and be forced to either return to bed or return to Caffe Riggio for more bawdy espresso sipping, chess and bloviating.

If the writer were to inhabit a full-fledged house, it could take as long as a half an hour after waking to actually commence writing. For example, upon waking, he must first run the gauntlet of hallways to get to the den. Then he must put the coffee on, turn on the computer, go to the bathroom, wait for the computer to boot up, go back into the kitchen to get a cup, get the coffee, walk back to the den, open the program, find his place, collect his thoughts. By that time, it's midnight, time to go back to bed.

STUNTED MOBILITY

The writer is a congenital rambler. If you are predisposed to be a writer at birth, you are also predisposed to wonder. After all, if a writer owns a house he will find himself in a position to have friends and entertain guest in said home. Writers are constantly looking for story ideas and the best can be found in the form of eccentric outsiders—often called weirdoes. If a writer can't just change his phone number, get a new apartment, or leave the universe, he's stuck. This prospect strikes fear in the hearts of many writer. It's okay for the writer to force others to be his friend, but it's absolutely unconscionable for someone he dislikes to invade his personal space. His preference is to run. Owning a house severely hampers that ability.

GARDENING FREIGHTENS HIM

No doubt writers have heard stories about savage, roving, bands of homeowners, hunting down garden slugs with cups of beer and drowning them to protect their little organic fiefdoms. But the writer cannot, in good conscious, participate in such a slaughter. His relationship with the slug is much too intimate. A writer knows this kind of repudiation. The slug is the writer's mascot, and buried in the bottom of the bureau drawer is his copy of David Greenberg's children's book *Slugs*, his favorite.

FAMILY IMPLICATIONS

If a writer buys a house, the writer must have a dog to go along with it. And, if a writer gets a dog, there must be kids to play with it. To get kids, the writer must find a woman to bear them. And so goes the Boolean loop. As evidenced in exhaustive research, the kid will then attempt to destroy the writer.

COFFEEHOUSE SEPARATION SYNDROME

Apartments, in many cases, provide convenient access to coffeehouses, seedy dive bars, and experimental theatres, where writers gather to burble about their apartments and such. Affordable homes, however, are usually on the fringe of civilization, on the outskirts of existence, and, unless you live in Sausalito or Boulder, you'll be forced to leave the city to purchase a home. That, to the writer, is nothing short of social decapitation and the death of cool.

HOME REPAIR INCOMPETENCE

Most writers also fear becoming contractors, and feel they'll be forced to use all sorts of hazardous chemicals and power tools against their will—not to mention that the writer's hands are soft, delicate, precision instruments, capable of stirring men's souls. The idea that an errant miter saw might mangle them is frightening to the writer. So, he'll do all he can to belay homeownership as long as possible, and will usually ONLY purchase a house when forced to by an insistent spouse. The exception is, of course, the how-to book writer. Those kinds of writers love building stuff. They build so they can write about it.

FRINGE EXISTANCE

The writer who is completely emerged in writing has little time for details, especially financially related ones. His past is a variable credit hornets nest, filled with default payments, overcharged credit cards, lost security deposits from abandoned apartments, repossessed cars, IRS liens, and perhaps a bankruptcy or two, which makes it difficult to get financing for a home. With today's technology, a mortgage company can track a person's history down to the last place they used the bathroom. It's harder to hide, so the writer must keep moving, lest he be found out.

SIX MONTHS OF DOWN TIME

Consider, too, what it takes to find a home. Searching alone involves hours and hours of weekends going to open homes, perusing classifieds, reviewing MLS printouts, driving around neighborhoods, and, in general, banging your head against a wall trying to find any kind of deal. All of this is a distraction from writing. The estimated three to six months it takes to find, purchase, and finally move into a house means excessive down time for the writer. This kind of down time might make the writer go berserk and run down the middle of the street wearing only a bear skin and wielding a spear while screaming, "I don't want to do this anymore!"

FEAR OF FURNITURE

Owning a home also means having to buy real furniture, like a bed, for example. Futons, beanbags, and generally crappy, second-hand, other people's rejects would no longer be appropriate. In most cool cities, it's difficult to find a home for under three hundred thousand dollars. And the furniture that was once befitting a 250 square foot studio no longer applies

FEAR OF ENTERING THE MAIN STREAM AND NOT BEING ABLE TO GET OUT AGAIN

Writers—particularly the very young ones and the extreme older ones who have fallen off the edge—absolutely, positively fear entering the main stream and losing their edge, even if they've fallen off of it. Buying a home means they might have to get a nice car to go with it, perhaps a Prius, Subaru or Hundai. They might even have to wear nice clothes to go with the car and the house. Life, there on after, will be an endless stream of purchasing things to go with things; things, I might add, any self acclaimed writer feels will suck his creativity right out of his brain. And it does happen.

The result of all these fears has lead writers to form perimeter defenses that are almost impenetrable; social support systems designed to praise apartment life and discourage home ownership. In some tight knit circles of writers, should the topic of owning property ever arise, the conversation may suddenly became uncomfortably stilted, and the instigator of said topic could, as is common in some cults, risk social "disassociation." After all, to write the writer must remain focused. To focus, the writer must surround himself with fruit for ideas. The apartment, in a dense urban setting, is the consummate breeding ground for creativity. The writer knows this, and any attempt to dislodge him from his habitat could lead to more intensified, spontaneous, gratuitous java sipping, spontaneous jabbering, and aggressive chess playing at Caffe Riggio.

Chapter 10
Writers and Taxes (Death and Writing)

I'm thinking about a story about a writer and taxes. The story involves the unsinkable battleship named the USS IRS, running silently in the night, big guns at the ready, searching for my little one-masted, 7-foot sloop called the Kismet. Their mission: to destroy me no mater what. A showdown is inevitable. It's a cold, windy night off the coast of San Francisco. The waves are beating against the Kismet as I train my binoculars on the dark horizon. Suddenly, I spot the eerie nautical lanterns skimming across the black waters just off my starboard bow. It's much bigger than I imagined. It spots me. I panic and start barking orders at my imaginary crew. The legal turrets with 10-inch guns turn in my direction. I have no where to go. All seems hopeless. My only option is to face off with the USS IRS and try to ram it and do some damage before I am blasted out of the water by the fear of complete financial annihilation. With the resoluteness of a bombardier beetle taking on a giant beetle-eating frog, I paddle feverishly towards the behemoth on a direct intercept course.

Closer. Closer. I reach ramming speed. Just before my boat slams into the starboard side of the USS IRS, I stand, salute, and sing the Harvard fight song as my destiny unfolds. CRASH! When my skiff rams the IRS, something strange happens. My little, insignificant, floating wood-splinter of a boat somehow manages to cripple the IRS. It retreats to its base; its efforts to destroy me frustrated. I limp back to shore to assess my situation. To my surprise, it appears I won the battle. I return, triumphant, to my two hundred and fifty square foot studio a hero, haggard and war torn, but at peace for the first time in a long time.

This story is true, dear friends. The original Star Wars movie—where a single X-wing fighter destroys the seemingly indestructible Death Star by exploiting its one weak spot—gave me enough hope and courage to face the IRS. In my case, I didn't destroy the IRS. I was, however, able to find the weak spot, keep them at bay, and eventually emancipate myself from their grip and take back my life and the ability to actually have "a genuine nice day." Herewith is the story of how it was done. This is the longer of my tales, so fetch some fresh Java and read ahead. Steady as you go.

My troubles began in 1985, the year of the Apple Macintosh computer. After a self-imposed artist's sabbatical (occurs after a writer gets tired of working real jobs) in London, England, I returning to Denver, Colorado, for a week to visit my sister Monique and my nephew Bernard and celebrate her birthday. With the money I had from my cashed-in Chevron stock, I then caught a seventy-five dollar, one-way flight to San Francisco. When I arrived, I stashed all my possessions (Four bags and my Remington Noiseless typewriter) into an airport locker and took a SAMTRANS bus to Daly City. There, I rented a room at the Mission Bell Hotel and planned my next move. This was to begin the last leap in a multi-year quest to get over the Rockies to the West Coast. I was 25 years old, and singularly focused on continuing my magazine publishing career in a place where they actually had magazines. Daily City was the last BART stop, so I took the train into downtown San Francisco to look for a cheap hotel, sign up with two temporary agencies and kiss the ground.

I found the Grand Central Hotel at Market and Vanness. It was a fleabag of a hotel that cost me $100 a week. I put up with the pounding on the door in the night, piss in the elevators and the sleazy hot sex-tub business in the basement because this was as good a start as any. It took two days to secure a temporary job through Kelly Temps as photo editor for Ortho Books (Chevron), a large publisher of gardening and home-improvement books. The walk to Chevron was an easy walk down Market Street from my hotel.

After two weeks, Ortho offered me an employment contract that included a five-figure income, more money than I'd ever seen in my life and three-times what I made as a Chevron geological librarian/underground performer/publisher/pianist in Denver. I would be working in Chevron's headquarters on the 36th floor at 575 Market Street. I enjoyed spectacular views by day and stimulating work, then walked the gauntlet of porno movie houses, tourist-trap shops and packed sidewalks of people who meandered hither and dither on my way back to the Grand Central.

Nights at the Grand Central were filled with screaming and arguing in the hallways and occasional pounding on my door. The sink in my room was the same rusty brown color as the carpet, and I could swear I felt something crawling on me while I slept. I wore a suit and tie to work, so I left quickly in the mornings. When I opened my room door, it smelled like everyone but me peed in the hallway instead of the shared bathroom.

I took to the San Francisco lifestyle very easily as if I was meant to be there. I worked 9 to 5 at the office, then hit the happy hours with my new friends. I lunched almost every day and began my precipitous intellectual and social foodie and publishing climb.

Two weeks later I earned enough money to checked out of the Grand Central and into the Blackstone Apartments, just a block away and a slight graduation from sleazy hotel to a roach-infested studio with shared bathroom down the hall. Money, like sand, slipped right through my fingers. But I was making enough to make the numbers work out. I ate out most nights, did night clubbing, event partaking, museum promenading, and gallery hopping. Two more apartment hops later landed me in the garage of a Victorian house in Hayes Valley. The garage was converted into an illegal three-bedroom apartment with a garage door entrance and plenty of space to thrive and entertain friends. I was feeling like things were really going my way.

My favorite pastime was hosting theme parties. I perfected the process with my friend Calvin Ranson at KSU, then in Denver years earlier. I continued that trend in San Francisco. My favorite was the Saint Valentine's Day massacre big band party. I figured out that most lunch spots downtown were closed on weekends, so if I told a manager I wanted to have a party on a Saturday night for 200 people who would buy lots of drinks, they usually said yes—with no charge for the space and a free case of champagne for starters. That was my little secret. Location secured, I settled on a theme and mailed invitations to all my friends. Most showed up.

Life seemed good on the outside, but in the closet, several serious problems were burgeoning, one of which involved the most dreaded acronym known to man, the I-R-S.

As a self-employed independent contractor editor and publisher, I was responsible for paying my own taxes. I, like many self-employed professionals, considered being a contractor a financial windfall. Each month I got a paycheck that reflected exactly what I made. No deductions. No frills. And, with the cost of goods, there simply wasn't enough to share with the government, lest I be forced to live like other people and perform that dreaded, arduous, exhausting task of saving money. Saving money involved being prudent, rational, and perhaps even making a budget and diligently sticking to it. That, I convinced myself, was absurd. So, instead of paying my estimated quarterly or annual taxes, I aggressively spent every penny I made. I was investing in my artistry after all. I would pay off any tax liabilities I accumulated when I was ready and had accumulated a financial armada. And, since I delayed even filing my taxes by, say, three years, I really had no idea what the implications were. Rumor had it that I was supposed to file a schedule C or something like that. Never happened. That was such a huge departure from my 1040 EZ filings in Denver, that I punted filing taxes yearly, convincing myself that all would be okay and I'd get to it when I got to it.

Unfortunately, it didn't quite work out that way. The IRS, you see, had no sympathy for my situation, or my art, and was not interested in my future earnings. They were singularly focused on one thing alone: bringing me to my knees and extracting what I owe NOW!

The Federal Government, I learned, was the most unforgiving and impatient creditor that exist, and they possessed the most sophisticated search and destroy infrastructure imaginable. By thinking as I did and making some rather bad financial assumptions, I found myself on the IRS Shit list A, a secret list of late-filing *rabid* citizens to seek out and destroy.

I eventually received a letter from the IRS. It read as follows:

Dear Mr. Quinton,

We noticed that you have not filed tax returns for...
Sincerely,

Rob Koblinsky
Senior Collections Specialist
IRS US Government

Here's what my mind heard:

Dear Mr. Quinton,

The jig is up. We know all about you. Time to get on your knees and pray to whatever God you worship. We're coming to take you away!

Sincerely,
The Holders of Your Future and Freedom in America
Your Powerful and Omnipotent IRS US Government – America The Beautiful

In Denver I was a geological librarian AND a law librarian for Chevron, so I knew my way around the federal tax code books. I went to the public library and re-familiarized myself with the income tax laws. I studied the tax statutes enough to know I could avoid criminal prosecution by filing accurate taxes and not lying. I could then only be guilty of lateness and stupidity. I also sought out some advice from my fellow contractors. After my exhaustive research, I filed all my taxes with the 1040 and the schedule C. After three years of contracting and having NO deductions, I incurred a total tax liability of over $14,000 to the IRS and $2,000 to the state. Late fees and penalties pushed that liability to over $20,000. The IRS intimidation campaign started immediately thereafter, and no matter how many successes or wins I had after that, the specter of those liabilities followed me around San

Francisco wherever I went like a turd on my psyche. The IRS and the state were not about to let me forget my financial obligation.

The IRS bills and letters arrived every two weeks on average. I occasionally peeked at them but mostly ignored them. The first IRS demands were sufficiently nasty and effectively intimidating. No matter what they said after that, this is what I read:

Dear Mr. Quinton,

You may have had a good day yesterday, but the purpose of this letter is to shit on your "good day" parade today. We are all powerful. We are everywhere. We will beat you down until you relent. And, if that doesn't work, we have the power to make sure you never have a fully joyful day ever. Plus, we'll take everything you own and, well—we need to say this Mr. Quinton—we will eat your family. By the way, this is your entire fault. You are a loser. Don't try to have a good day. Remember, we're always watching.

Sincerely,
Purveyors of Doom
Your Powerful and Omnipotent IRS America - The Great Land of Freedom
P.S. I'm having a great day today.

Subsequent notices got nastier (if that's possible) and more threatening. In so many words, they said they would destroy me, my family, my friends, everything I cherished, and even bring me back from the grave and taunt me if I tried to die without paying. Somebody somewhere had to pay the taxes I owed, and they would not relent until the bill was satisfied. I filed the demand letters away in a deep, dark drawer and went about my day.

I carried on with my lifestyle with zeal. I continued to throw outrageous parties every quarter, eat great food, and sported stylish vintage clothing (pleated and cuffed wool slacks, pastel colored rayon shirts, wing tips, vintage wool Brooks Brothers sport jackets, original Stetson Fedora, worn slightly tipped) and a vintage Stevens wool herringbone trench. I was always in the right place at the right time, quick with a quip, and ready to rock and roll 'til dawn. I was the master of illusions.

In reality, I was so deep in denial. I even found it difficult to be honest in my journals. Journals are supposed to be sacred places to pencil only truths. I lied to myself in my journals. If I did mention taxes, I did so in a vague, cryptic way that sounded more like the writings of a paranoid schizophrenic. Here's a sample:

"...*got another envelope today, they're very persistent. But it's okay, they can't find me. And I need the money to live.*"

"...*the artist life is difficult, especially with THEM sending me notices all the time.*"

"...*could be time to get out of dodge. They're coming, I know they are. GOD, if you exist, please don't let them get me.*"

    It wasn't unusual for me to challenge God to prove his or her existence and make the IRS go away. Nothing every changed though, so some of my faith diminished proportionately over the years as my tax bill mounted.

    After a while, I became really paranoid. I was forced, like Salmon Rushdie, to go into financial hiding in order to keep a couple of steps ahead of the IRS goons. I left Ortho, worked short-term contract jobs, kept a P.O. box, and continued to keep very little money in my accounts. To a certain extent, I kept a low financial profile thinking that might help. My strategy worked. But they always found me. One of my checking accounts got "sucked" by the IRS. They got $25 bucks. Assholes.

    Eventually, I made several fateful mistakes that forced me into a box. First, got a driver's license after close to 10 years without having one. Second, I began living with someone I was romantically involved with, which made it more difficult to run. Third, I drank myself into oblivion to forget. Next, my book about San Francisco lunch spots was a hit and I was showing up in newspaper articles and on radio and television shows regularly. And lastly, I entered into a corporate partnership and founded the successful *Commercial Property Guide* and the *Bay City Guide*. All of those things further forced me to stay put for at least a year, and that year was all the IRS needed to get a lock on me like a guides missle.

    During that last year in hiding as Vice President and Executive Editor of Guide Publishing Group, the IRS (or the humans it had possessed) would leave vague, ominous messages on my answering machine. For example, some messages went as follows:

"*Mr. Quinton, could you please call Phyllis concerning your tax liability.*"
"*Mr. Quinton, we really need to talk about your tax bills.*"

"Mr. Quinton, it's very important that you call us immediately concerning your taxes."

I continued to ignore the messages and usually erased them immediately. They're getting closer. My girlfriend and I were living in a fabulous apartment at Oak and Baker. Not much of a view, but lots of windows and a few blocks from the Haight. We had talked about moving to a two bedroom apartment so we could have an extra room for an office (she was a graphic designer). So, when I woke up one morning and found the business card of an IRS agent stuck on my mailbox with a note saying, "Please contact us immediately," I freaked out. A few months later we had found a two-bedroom apartment with the sliver of a Golden Gate Bridge view in Pacific Heights, a few blocks away from the Fairmont Hotel. We were paying twice as much money, but it was nice, and I was temporarily safe again. I had a new address, a new phone number, and a new P.O. box. Maybe this time I could put enough distance between the IRS and myself. Maybe they would never find me again.

The calm would not last long. Within that one-year period, the stress wreaked havoc on my life. I became more of a fanatical drinker, a talent I nurtured over the year. I was a half-alcoholic; psychologically—not physically—addicted. Alcohol was a crutch, you see, that allowed me to maintain that sense of romance while all was crumbling around me. A gin martini, Nat King Cole on the jukebox, and a dark wood-paneled bar like John's Grill, were all I needed to feel significant, important, and cool. My body, on the other hand, hated alcohol and begged me to quit on a regular basis. But drinking was the perfect deterrent to responsibility. It didn't allow time for battles or attending to the tedium of paying IRS bills and whatnot. While drinking, romance was all that mattered. I was not destitute, by any means. In fact, I was doing quite well and mostly a responsible adult. Our magazines were thriving. I was on the tourism PR A-list, so I received invitations to everything. My girlfriend and I lived like celebrities but rarely had to pay for these indulgences. Our magazines had tens of thousands of dollars in trade at our disposal, so my partner and I rented yachts to cruise the Sacramento River on weekends, sail the Bay regularly in 60 foot sailboats, and we ate at the finest restaurants. Public relations companies provided review tickets and guest passes to the opera, symphony, art openings, and political events. We rubbed shoulders with Mayor Art Agnos and the editors of *San Francisco Magazine* and the two newspapers. My restaurant guide was very popular, so I was a minor celebrity. But no matter how much access and success I had, the ghost of the IRS followed me wherever I went.

My walk to work and home every day was nothing short of spectacular. I strolled over to Hyde Street and followed the cable car on Hyde Street over the hill to Union Street, taking in view of Alcatraz, the Golden Gate Bridge and Marin. In the evenings when going home, I sometimes walked up Van Ness, hanged a left at Market Street, and ducked into John's Grill at Powell and Market Street. There, my favorite bartender Ray would greet me and make my favorite drink without asking. I drank a strong gin martini with a twist of lemon and five olives. That way, I could have an appetizer and a drink at the same time. After a couple strong martinis, I would usually go a couple blocks to Tad's for a half-spit-roasted chicken, baked potato and salad for $4.99. Our magazines had an account at Wolfgang Puck's restaurant and Kuleto's across the street, and I could eat there for free if I wanted to, but I preferred to pay $4.99 for a classic meal and a Budweiser that reminded me of a home-cooked meal. Fancy food was great but it got a little old after awhile. It was exhausting have to say, "This is fabulous" all the time. Sometimes I just wanted to eat plain, good food without all the frills. Know what I mean? I was feeling confused and alone.

Before the IRS found me again, I was already tired of the running and the drinking. Fortunately, two significant events (aside from all the organs in my body fervently protesting my alcohol abuse) inspired me to quit drinking cold turkey.

The first occurred in downtown San Francisco at Gio's restaurant. As a restaurant reviewer, editor, and gadabout, I was well known and accepted at many of San Francisco's finer establishment. These were relationships I valued. They were part of the romance, the scenario, and there were some truly fine, compassionate people involved. Typically, my only obligation as a customer in these establishments was to visit, bring my friends, be no less than riveting, and, when all was said and done, tip the waiter or bartender well.

The evening in question was a Friday happy hour. I spent nearly five hours at Gio's drinking martinis and white wine, eating sautéed meatballs, fried cheese balls, and beanie weenies. Giovani Constable was a friend, a confidant and an all-around good guy. He hosted one of my biggest Saint Valentine's Day gangster parties (and a few years later my wedding party). He also seemed like a godfather to me. He looked out for me. Around 10 p.m. I donned my wool trench, my Stetson, said my goodnights, held my chin high, and strode (never staggering) to the MUNI stop on Market Street. It was a beautiful San Francisco night. The moon was full. The air was chilled and misty.

Lights from the buildings created an array of multicolored neon-like hues. That was the scene I loved. Even during my absolute lowest moments, that scene of the moon shining behind the Transamerica tower and reflecting on the bay waters made everything seem romantic.

While waiting for the bus on Market Street, I began to feel queasy. After a few minutes of this sensation, I was sure I was going to throw up. No semi-socialite in dapper duds in his right mind could possibly throw up in a public place in downtown San Francisco. I was just a few blocks from the Chronicle offices where famed columnist Herb Caen worked. He was a huge fan of my popular restaurant guidebook. Fortunately, San Francisco's many alleyways provide ideal, private, and sacred puking grounds for the social elite. That's what alleys were for, right. I dashed down second street, ducked in the alley behind C&R clothiers, and there, right across from the stately Chevron World Corporate Headquarters, proceeded to blow chunks for what seemed like hours.

While puking, it was difficult to maintain some dignity, and not lose that sense of romance I so valued. Not to mention, it was impossible to keep it from getting on my shoes. There I was, alone in a dark alley, puking my guts out to save my life. I was forced to ask myself what I wanted my legacy to be; what I wanted my children to know about this great city and me. Did this activity befit a man with any kind of self-respect? Would I relate this moment to my children? Would I puke so violently that I would come out of my nostrils? There was a moment—even if fleeting—of profound introspection and revelation. For the first time in my life, I acknowledged that puking in the alley was disgusting. With the gong of the midnight clock of the Ferry Plaza Building Tower, I was overcome by a deepening sense of foreboding.

Speaking of clocks, the IRS clock of doom was ticking. They were getting closer. *Tick. Tick. Tick. Tick.* Garnishment notices systematically went to all past employers. *Tick. Tick. Tick. Tick.* Did I have time to make my millions and get out? *Tick. Tick. Tick. Tick.* They put a lien on my Merrill Lynch Capital Builder account. *Tick. Tick. Tick. Tick.* The notices came more frequently to my P.O. Box. *Tick. Tick. Tick. Tick.* Penalties and interest mounted. *Tick. Tick. Tick. Tick.* The strain caused the break-up of my relationship. *Tick. Tick. Tick. Tick.* I moved out of our swanky Pacific Heights apartment and into a tiny lower Knob Hill studio apartment. *Tick. Tick. Tick.* Drinking was calculated avoidance behavior. I could affirm my happiness staggering home after raucous evening of spirited conversation with friends at The Vesuvio Cafe in North Beach. *Tick. Tick. Tick.*

Event number two took place in 1989 on my 30th birthday. At that point, I was living in a studio in the zone between hoity-toity Knob Hill and the Tenderloin, that seamy city underbelly. I dubbed it the Knoberloin or Tenderknob. I decided to give a 70s disco party at Ray's bar on Larkin, a couple of blocks from my studio. It was, to say the least, the seediest of the seedy bars, and a hotbed of alcoholism.

The owner, Ray, was a raving alcoholic who kept a Budweiser in his hand from morning till nightfall. His face was harsh and bloated, and his skin was red and askew from years of sucking down liquor of all types. He lived in the back of the bar, with his wife, who suffered from Alzheimer's, and normally (if you could say that) sat at the bar all day, saying, "I love my Raymond. I love my Raymond." I genuinely liked Ray and his crowd. There were a lot of guys who'd gone over the edge, and since I was a fringer, on my way over, I could identify them.

I wanted to honor Ray by having my birthday party at his establishment, and showing him I was one of his kind. I rented the back room for $200, minimally decorated the room, bought a pink polyester suit, brought in a record player, some big speakers, and on that fateful evening about 100 of my closest friends showed up in polyester, paisley, platforms and such to celebrate my birthday. We packed the place and danced to music from the Bee Gees, KC and the Sunshine Band, and Rick James till 2 a.m. It was one hell of a party.

When the party was over, we cleaned up, packed up the stereo, thanked Ray and said goodnight to he and his wife, who promptly responded, "I love my Ray Ray." A friend helped me cart all the stuff up the hill to my studio. I passed out on my futon listening to the Bill Evan's Paris concert album and swimming in an ocean of perceived romance.

The next morning I awoke to a devastating, paralyzing hangover. I literally could not move. The most I could do was watch my 4-inch black and white TV all day and recite, "though I walk through the valley of the shadow of death, I will fear no evil..." Last rites, I felt, were appropriate. In truth, I probably should have been admitted to a hospital. Ninety percent of my brain had been killed, and my liver, no doubt, was in complete failure.

That was the first time the pain of a terrible hangover was so crippling and real. I felt as though someone was eating my brain with pitchfork. I couldn't walk. If I moved, I would double up in pain. Aspirin didn't help either. What I needed was to be put out of my misery.

A few days later I got the pictures back from the party. They were more shocking and disturbing than the hangover. There I stood, in a pink polyester leisure suit. I looked bloated, plastered, and sad. I looked a lot like my dad, who, by the time he reached his late 40's, had no control over his life. Alcohol had taken over. I stared at that picture for hours, then quit drinking on the spot.

I knew the bomb was about to go off. If I had not stopped drinking, it would have gone off in my face, and I would have had no recourse but to leave the state, go as far as I could from my problems, cover my shit with branches, and wait for them to find me again. I would be a financial fugitive and could never build any close ties, never marry, never own anything traceable, and always be ready to leave at a moment's notice…like The Accountant.

The staging ground for my showdown with the IRS was set. I was a partner in a corporation, drinking rarely and people's lives and livelihoods now depended on me. I could not run or I would have to keep running forever. It was a beautiful, sunny, spring afternoon when my partner called a meeting with me to discuss something of great import. It seemed the IRS was knocking at his door with a garnishment order. The wind shot out of my sails and embarrassment set in. I wanted to stand up and run from the meeting. I felt sure I would be kicked out of the corporation and all I had worked for would be ruined. But that was not the case. My partner, Drew Patterson, was no stranger to dealing with the IRS. He was empathetic and said, "Hey, Ray, I'm in your corner. We'll fight this thing together. You're my friend, partner and part owner of this corporation. We have the resources to fight this. Get a lawyer. The corporation will pay for it. Take the time you need to deal with court, and we'll get past this."

I almost teared up. It didn't take much for me to be reminded that there are a lot good people in the world, and I'm not the only who's ever had problems. Drew's wife, Athena, was even more surprising. She walked into our meeting, looked at me, smiled and said in her usual, blunt very French accent, "Those sons of de bitches urnt wort a sheet. Tell dem to kees yur ass. Here's a chek fur de lewyers. Feel in de amount and de name. See u latter Rrrramond." Then she was gone. This was my A-team and my secret weapon. It seemed a little support was all I needed to forge this battle.

The IRS lien called for me to immediately surrender 80 percent of my wages and somehow live off of whatever was left over, which amounted to approximately $150 per month. That was motivation enough to attempt to resolve this and every problem in my life somehow. This was one of the biggest, a problem that was clearly interwoven into many other problems I had, and a problem that begged an immediate resolution.

Filing for bankruptcy was an option I entertained several times, but the idea of it seemed distasteful. The implications, based on several horror stories I'd heard, were also frightening to me. To file for bankruptcy meant I was ruined, financially insolvent, destitute, AND, meant I would be forced to take my place in the disreputable hall of those with bad credit. All these things represented failure. The alternative, however, was far too frightening. I could not live off of $150 per month.

After thinking my situation through, I conceded that reality had to prevail. I was in the precarious position of having nothing to lose. Be that as it may, what others thought of me was inconsequential. Either I turned and faced my demons, or they would eat me alive. I had no excuses anymore. Since I'd tackled drinking, I could not tarry on down to the local bar, slam down a few glasses of Chardonnay, and—in my euphoric state of torpor—covince myself everything was okay.

That evening, in exasperation, I bought the Bay Guardian and looked in the classifieds under bankruptcy lawyers. I had seen the ads before. They ran every week. The same lawyers. CHEAP BANKRUPTCY. CALL 1800BANKRUPT TODAY! I gritted my teeth and called a few of the numbers listed. Most of the lawyers I talked to sound like thugs, or I was transferred to some anonymous voicemail system that directed me to leave a message. "Please state specifically what kind of bankruptcy you wish to file," they said. I couldn't do that. That was too much like putting in an order at McBankruptcy. Finally, I called Stephen Johnson, attorney at law. He answered the phone and explained my plight.

Johnson seemed sincere, straightforward and up front about the cost. The retainer was reasonable, and I could pay off the remainder of the balance in installments. He could also file the petition the next day, which would release our corporation from the lien against my wages and prevent all collections thereafter while we met to prepare a formal petition.

I got lucky. Mr. Johnson turned out to be a Godsend. His office was in Tiburon, a quick, beautiful bus ride across the Golden Gate Bridge into Marin County. His associates were Marinesque activists and vegans who wore Birkenstocks and Guatemalan fashions to the office. Visiting a bankruptcy lawyer was never so mellow.

My options were clear. I had to bite the bullet and file for bankruptcy or face a life on the run, perhaps eventually, a life in the streets. It would cost me $400 for everything, even if I had to file a chapter 7 and a chapter 13. I wrote out the check for the full amount, handed it to Mr. Johnson, then caught the bus back to San Francisco.

As I crossed over the Golden Gate Bridge to San Francisco, I marveled at the beauty of the brilliant red, yellow and gold streams of light shining over a bank of fog about to engulf the towers of the bridge. A tear trickled down the corners of my eyes. "To hell with it all," I said to myself, "I saving my life."

The rest of the paperwork took a couple of weeks. Once all my debts were consolidated and tallied, I owed close to $30,000 in taxes, penalties, business debts, and personal debts. The strategy was to file a Chapter 7 first. This form of bankruptcy was designed to forgive and erase debts. This included all taxes that were three years old or older. All other secured or unsecured debts, regardless of age, would be forgiven as well. That effectively erased about $10,000 of my debt. The lion's share of my IRS debt, however, was not dischargable, which meant some $20,000 remained after the judge's final order.

The initial court appearance initiated me into a private club called bankruptcy court (once called debtor's court). The court was filled with all sorts of colorful characters. There were professional people, working class people, parents with children, young, old, unsavory types, and scam artist. Since I was pretty far down on the alphabet, I had to sit around for four hours awaiting my turn and listening to their stories. You could easily distinguish the people who were sincere from the ones who filed bankruptcies for a living. Bankruptcy regulars usually wore gold rings and fancy suits. Their claimed expenses were outrageously high and income incredibly low. The judge, surprisingly, treated everyone fairly. Everyone, whether saint or scum, was entitled to equal treatment under the law. We were all citizens, kin in debtor's court. And we all hoped the judge would not have any embarrassing question about our financial affairs when our case number came up. And we all hoped *no* debtors showed up to protest our filing and complicate things.

My moment in the hot seat came and went quicker than I had imagined. My lawyer, so it seems, forgot to give the judge a copy of my file. My court date was rescheduled and I was thoroughly embarrassed. I called Mr. Johnson and raked him (nicely) over the coals, and he assured me that my file would be in the court the next time. A month later, the same scenario was repeated. After a four-hour wait, and listening to all sorts of sad stories, the judge finally stamped my case approved.

That was round one. Round two came a few months later, after my Chapter 7 was discharged. The judge officially ruled that $20,000 in self-employment taxes and penalties was not dischargable. And the IRS wasted no time sending out their liens and calculating more penalties and interest. I was forced to play my hand, to bring out the big guns so to speak. I called Mr. Johnson, and told him we needed to "do the 13." By that point, it was easy for me. This was my second tour of duty. I was a seasoned veteran. I could sit for hours without developing butt cramps, and I made sure my file was there. I knew this was the only way to keep the IRS at bay, and being a quick study, I knew that this was all legal and that I was NOT a bad person for using the law as it was meant to be used to provide some financial relief. The irony was that that relief was from the government that writes the law.

The IRS agents were clever opponents, though, and countered my strategy with a few tricks of their own. Since I was a marked file in the IRS computer, the system automatically dredged up everything it could find on my tax history (with a little help from humans, of course). For example, in the early eighties, I neglected to file taxes for a few years. The IRS, searched my records, discovered the missing returns. They filed those missing tax returns for me based on employer withholdings and estimated that I owed them some $4,000 in additional taxes. I was forced send away for ancient w-2's and tax forms for 1981-82. I did so, filed the *real* taxes, and came up with numbers that showed the IRS owed me about a thousand dollars. I was awash with glee, but they quickly attached that amount and subtracted it from my owed balance.

They weren't finished yet. Out of the blue, I received a demand for copies of that current year's tax returns. The demand came from the IRS special Bankruptcy task force in San Francisco. The demand stated that if I didn't file the returns within 10 days, they threatened to ask the judge to throw out my bankruptcy petition. That would clear them to do their favorite dance, lien, attach and collect. I hand-delivered the returns to them. My tax liability for that year was $180. That amount was added to my Bankruptcy petition. When all was said and done, my monthly settlement payment was $418 dollars a month for a year. I paid diligently and with enthusiasm. A year later, my case was discharged, and I got a refund of $418 for making one payment too many. I also received a nice letter from the honorable Judge Duncan Kester thanking me for being so consistent and for concluding the case.

I weathered the frustrations, stress, and social implications of filing *two* bankruptcies in three months. I fought off the IRS and won—so to speak. I managed to keep myself from living a life on the run as so many writers before me have done. But was it an empty victory?

I'm sure my credit report was probably used as a test file for TRW trainees. That, however, seemed a small price to pay to be able to sleep at night. You can lead a happy, fulfilled life without credit if you know how to make and use money. I knew how to do both. I did, in fact, learn to live better without credit cards than most people with credit cards. I was frugal, paid cash for everything, and realized that you can always find your way back if you're determined to. On the other hand, depressions, fear, anxiety, alcohol, are all things, that will cripple a life, and make it difficult to get through a single day with any amount of optimism.

In spite of having filed two bankruptcies, I've had several successful businesses, AND gotten refunds from the IRS almost every year since. I've even got a little cocky and hired an accountant who kept the IRS and me honest. I paid my taxes religiously and also took advantage of any deductions my family or my businesses deserved. You might say I become a deduction zealot, and rightly so. I'm no longer afraid of the big bad wolf, the IRS.

On my first coffee rendezvous with my future first and x-wife, I told her I drank rarely, was financially working my way back from a bankruptcy, and I was never happier. Six months later, we were married at San Francisco City Hall and had a fabulous party at Gio's. Almost six years and two children later, we had moved to Portland. My wife and I were buying our second home, paid off the loan on our $12,000 truck, and we owed very few people, including the IRS, anything. A few years later I was packing in nearly $80,000 a year as a corporate marketing manager at Hollywood Video's 2600 stores and. We bought an even bigger house because my credit score was hovering around 800. There is life after bankruptcy. But, to a certain extent, there is not much hope, in many people's situations, without it.

While filing bankruptcy is nothing to take lightly or necessarily be proud of, it is a legal, justifiable option when—because of stupid errors in judgment—no other options are available. I didn't have family or friends to bail me out. So I did what I thought I had to do. I learned from the experience and never hope to repeat it again. The final entry in my journal on this matter, some six years later, went as follows:

"...I rammed the steely battleship, the USS IRS. My insignificant little sloop impaired the enemy's ability to destroy me, as it surely would have done had I tried to run. I feel no remorse in doing what I have done. I could not have done less. I realize, too, it is unfair to characterize the IRS as a bully. After all, they were just doing their job. But it is and always will be true that the IRS is the nematode, preying on unsuspecting artists. The writer is particularly vulnerable because he is

singular focused on writing and rarely imagines creating great works of art AND paying millions of dollars in taxes too. We toil thanklessly for most of our lives trying to make a little money at our craft and make the world a better place. Once we make it, we must then give most of it away. That doesn't seem right. The writer, too, being naturally contemptuous of religion and government, must resist a little. We, after all, are the conscious of the people. If we do not protest, and articulate so, perhaps one day, instead of paying 40 percent of our earnings on taxes, we'll pay 90 percent. What was that guys name who talked about "taxation without representation." We ought not forget about that guy. Anyway, I'm thinking about a writer and taxes; a writer who faced the beast and won. At this juncture, I most quote those words made famous by the effervescent MC Hammer, "Can't Touch This."

Chapter 11
WANTED: ANYONE WHO CAN WRITE ANYTHING NOW!!!!

Societal memory is short. The memory of pundits is even shorter. In the past 75 years, many have forgotten that a great writer posses a skill that can change the world. *Uncle Tom's Cabin* didn't end slavery but it sure had a significant impact. Humans need ideas to believe in. Writers can corral the right ideas to believe in and movie a society to change… AND writers can INSTANTLY earn unlimited pools of cash. BULLY!! THE HELL YOU SAY!! Yes, it's true. This is no infomercial. The writer-value cycle is on an up-tick. A good-writer is once again moving towards being revered, redeemed and respected. Corporations are currently DESPARATE to hire anyone with a communications degree of any kind who can turn a phrase and make their business look and sound intelligent. The new writointellectual renaissance is rising up alongside the social-intellectual bell-curve, and the writer is seeing a new emergence of respect, credibility and significance. The problem is that no one has told the writers of the world yet.

This is not a trend that developed overnight, mind you. It took nearly 20 years for this phenomenon to finally materialize. Within that span of time, the writer experienced the lowest approval level in the history of civilization. Let me explain.

In 1981 when I graduated from the great American institution of Kansas State University, writing jobs were few and far between. Granted, there was a major recession going on, but that wasn't a significant factor in the writing market. Publishing of all types was considered an exclusive club at one point, so millions wanted to get in and get to the top but few doors were opening. In the 80s, editing and publishing was an exclusive intellectual country club, propagating itself for its own sake. Editors and publishers tended to look down on new writers and other humans and forced them to grovel and prostrate themselves before they would let them in. That groveling and prostrating would continue for 15 to 20 years before writers could have full access and make any serious money and achieve what the industry called "respect." Or, school, social class and race determined your progress in the industry. Sound familiar?

Writers—particularly newspaper reporters—ranked somewhere between hospital orderlies and fry cooks. Reporters also received similar wages—the lowest wage possible. Most publications figured they could go to the five-and-dime and buy writers right off the shelf, like a common painkiller. Common thinking was: Why pay them? Why coddle them? Why even acknowledge that they spent four years in college learning their trade? Publishers figured they had the world on a string and they were sitting on a rainbow. There were writers lining up to be reporters. This was the downside of *Superman* phenomenon.

Finally—and this is the biggest insult of them all—publishers were making millions on advertising but would not allow reporters (whom they considered the field works of the industry) the dignity of an honest wage for food shelter, reliable transportation and a hope of a professional future.

Come to think of it, the beginning journalist often made less money than a fry cook...and the fry cook could progress to assistant manager in a week if they showed up and proved reliable. To show you the gross injustices and indignities the writer endured, consider this: The average starting journalist wrote stories that shaped and molded the community, and, in some cases, the world. The average fry cook shaped and molded fat, greasy, vain-clogging burgers, served with thick adhesive-laden cream of vegetable soup resin, and typically didn't give a damn about the community. The average journalist kept politicians in check and protected the rights of citizens, while the average fry cook often didn't bother to vote because they considered all politicians scum. Finally, the journalist often could not afford to eat a greasy over-fried, faux-chino egg-foo-young incarnation of a meal because he usually spent his own money doing stories and trying to keep his aerosol can sprayed primer-grey Datsan assault vehicle running on the three remaining pistons.

In 1981 the beginning wage for a journalist was about $6,000 per year, if you were lucky to get a paying job (most first-year grads volunteered for internships or worked for insurance companies). That's approximately $3.35 per hour. We were told in college not to expect more than that. We were told to become stringers first and hope we got hired on as a staff reporter after a few years. But becoming a stringer meant spending hours and hours on stories and maybe getting paid 3 cents a word if one story was accepted. Since a 10,000 word story was usually carved (with a chain saw) down to 100 words, that meant the writer earned $3 for spending 6,000 hours putting together the alleged story. The math weighed heavily in the publishers' favor.

Being a writer or writer/journalist was a humbling, humiliating experience, and many of our most talented writers refused to bow to this system of subservient, indentured employment. It was degrading, and not conducive to promoting healthy self-esteem. The early 80s were indeed a dark time for writers. A few were getting filthy rich in real estate, while the others—in frustration—looked towards masters degrees (so they could teach), other professions (so they could get paid), or EST self-esteem workshops (so they could be happy). Some even became doctors and lawyers. I don't blame them. Doctors made way more money.

Others writers marched unwillingly towards corporate communications, which, at that time, was considered the ultimate cop-out. If you uttered the word public relations in a room of journalist, they would all stop, look in your direction, stare, and then scream one of those high-pitched squeals the pod-people squealed in *Return of the Body Snatchers*. In their eyes you were no longer human. You were the enemy.

As a public relations representative, the writer could at least, afford to eat, buy cloths, drive reliable transportation, and could afford a real apartment. He didn't have to live in a boarding house with psychos behind every door, or in a house with a bunch of 50-something burnt out journalist trying to develop a sitcom called *Friends: The Next Generation*. So much writing talent was sucked into the corporate world in the late 80's that a talent black hole evolved in the world of journalism. Journalism graduates wised up. Since there was no math required to graduate with a journalism degree, students could breeze through four years, graduate and be guaranteed a management position with companies like GM or Delco starting at $60,000 per year. With all due respect, the only writers left actually writing—with some exceptions—were those found at the bottom of the barrel, still optimistic or broke, and many devoid of any experience or passion for the trade. Publications had to take what they could get. And it wasn't a pretty sight. There was pandemonium.

Then publications started dropping like flies. Buyouts. Sellouts. Mergers. Lawsuits. Rampant alcoholism. Cocaine use. Sex in the sidebars. Hemorrhaging typos. Sloppy leads. Absence of elements of style. Editors going bonkers. Lack of subscribers. NO GOOD WRITERS TO BE FOUND ANYWHERE WHO WERE WILLING TO BE ABUSED FOR A PITTANCE INDEFINATELY!

Zruuuuuuuupppppppttffffzzzzz!!!!!!! It was 1997. Things were suddenly very different. Better. Take a deep breath. Do some trance dancing. Writers were getting rich by the busload as partners in creative agencies, writing massive amounts of content for web sites, CDROMS and other digital products!!!!

Between 1985 and 1997 things were turning right side up again for writers. A communications degree actually meant something again. People started realizing that good communications are the cornerstone of our society, and, yes, you *can* be trained to do it better than anyone else. They also started to realize that you couldn't just yank a passer-by off the street and say, "write me a great story or article or marketing materials—just communicate something, anything." That attitude cost many publications readers. And the lawsuits that resulted from the irresponsibility of the early 80s were astounding. Many good writers established professional careers writing for large corporate publications. Yes, folks, corporate communications became legitimate writing; respected and desirable. Journalism grads questioned the wisdom of writing about car accidents, pet stories, and sleazy politicians for the first 15 years of their professional careers and wondered if there would even be newspapers or magazines around by 2025. They used to say, "you'll never get rich as a writer." But that's was no longer true.

Out of desperation, newspapers in particular stooped so low as to place advertisements for reporters in the classifieds of other newspapers. Egad! That never happened before. They offered bundles of cash, benefits, cars, expense accounts and a whole plethora of other incentives just to find a competent reporter. There were and still are few takers. Today, corporate communications is king of the hill, and writers can earn first-year lawyer or engineer wages. Imagine that, graduating with a degree in English or journalism and getting a corporate writing or editing job that starts at $75,000 per year. That, for many writers, was better than winning the lottery. If you work consistently at that rate for 20 years, you could earn your first million by the time you're 45 years old. Then you can do what many doctors, lawyers or engineers do, retire, drop out to write a novel, start a software company, or invest in real estate and live happily ever after. That was not an option for the writers of yore.

If you're one of those writers who has not yet realized that there's a gold mine (a real one) out there waiting for you in corporate communications, wake up. You no longer have to be abused for your art unless you want to. OCEANS of cash are waiting for you in the world of communications. *STEP RIGHT UP! HURRY! HURRY! WRITERS WANTED! WE'RE GIVING CASH AWAY TODAY!*

Chapter 12
How to Be a Publisher 101

I saw Citizen Cane when I was in grade school. I know this sounds cliché, but it left such an impression on me that over the years something inside me kept repeating, "Be a publisher. Be a publisher." Or was it saying, "Rosebud." Whatever the case, by the time I was 16 I determined that I was definitely going to be a publisher. That was a fine thing to want to be. I soon realized, however, that I had a problem that would raise serious doubts about this aspiration. You see, dear friends, I was mathematically incompetent. This could have been a naturally occurring intellectual phenomenon. Or it could have been a math deficiency exacerbated by Catholic-scholastic trauma exacerbated by the nuns in grade school and by Mr. Laski in middle and high schools.

Let's explore this phenomenon a bit more. Mr. Laski was the terrible middle and high school math slash basketball coach slash track coach slash assistant principal slash algebra instructor. Sister Theresa was the grade school math slash history slash English slash everything else teacher. For some unknown reason both Sister Theresa and Mr. Laski had some obsession about calling on me to solve math problems *out loud* in class. I was sure they were targeting me. And there was nothing I could do. When called on in class to solve a problem on the board, I was forced to stand up, stare at the board and reluctantly announce, "I don't know." "It's simple," Mr. Laski would sometimes say. Then, he'd explain the answer while I stood there. Then he'd roll his eyes and say—with disgust—"You can sit down now Quinton." By that time, I was soaked with sweat and nearing tears. Brian Pollack, the class bully—and an individual whom I had an ongoing feud with—sat behind me sniggering uncontrollably under his breath, enjoying my public humiliation.

When confronted with math, I panicked. Erratic breathing. Profuse sweating. My thoughts turned to mashed potatoes and all logic and reasoning shut down. Occasionally, I stuttered, babbled incoherently, fall to the ground then curled into a fetal position. Math could NOT be part of my career framework.

After seeing *Citizen Kane* I had my first adolescent career AHA moment. Journalism was the yellow brick road to success. I work could with words and ideas for the rest of my life. No Math! Eureka! With that idea in mind, I charged forward singing—in my finest Broadway musical voice—*"Grab your pica pole young man and Be a publisher. With your pica pole in hand BEEEEE a publisher. Dance your way to fortune and fame. Your proportion wheel will show you the game. Be a publisher today!"*

It looked easy in *Citizen Kane*. But Hearst and I had nothing in common. My origins were quite bizarre compared to his. I sucked at math. I didn't read a novel until I was in ninth grade. For the record, reading *Tom Sawyer* out loud in class in middle school at St. Xavier didn't count. All I remember from that experience was hearing *nigger this* and *nigger that* and *nigger, nigger, nigger, nigger, nigger.* Each time the word nigger was read, everyone looked up at me. That was not reading. That was torture—very uncomfortable and humiliating. After that experience, I did not want to "read" any more novels. I, instead, loved reading *Time Life* books on everything. I loved encyclopedias and books on Greek mythology. And I loved joking around and movies, especially *Jason and the Argonauts*. That was the profile of a kid who wanted to be a publisher. It all seemed highly unlikely save for a series of *fortunate* events.

During the summer of 1976 I was lucky enough to participate in the summer *Upward Bound* program for inner-city kids (Yes, Junction City had an inner city—about two blocks south of downtown). Kansas State University hosted the program. Part of the program included living in the student dorms, working part-time in the cafeteria, taking two college level courses—*English 101* and *Human Growth and Development*. Lyman Baker was my English professor and Judy Knolting was my HG&D professor. I aced both courses and both professors were exceptional and encouraging. Dr. Baker said I had some natural writing talents. Dr. Knolting said I was really perceptive and smart. That was all I needed. It was easier to return to St. Xavier knowing I had a way out. That, along with the supported of my art teacher, Mrs. Maloney, and my friend and mentor Fr. Frank Coady, made my last year in Junction City almost bearable. I spent the rest of my time with best-friend Kevin Willmott. Being a publisher seemed reachable.

It was after that summer at Kansas State that I decided to re-think my attitude about novels. I read *Catcher in the Rye*, which led a profound resurgence and respect for reading novels. Then I read the *Summer of 42* that same year, and was hooked thereafter.

After graduating from high school, I attended a college that was the farthest away from Junction City. That way I could feel like I traveled somewhere and still pay in-state tuition. I packed my 4-door, 66 Dodge "grandma car" Dart and, like the pioneers of yore, headed 150 miles west to Fort Hays State University in Hays, Kansas. I started my college career studying journalism there in the fall of 1977, then transferred back to Kansas State in 1978 to finish my degree by 1981.

The journalism departments at both schools churned out small-town newspaper journalist, agricultural writers and editors like sausages at a hog farm. The KSU program was excellent; not as famous as the one at Kansas University, but the school sported some exceptional instructors. Most professors were accomplished writers and editors for newspapers like the *Salina Journal* or the *Wichita Eagle Beacon*. Some had tenure at such prestigious magazines as the *Wheat Monthly* or *Corn Review*. Some professors made it out of Kansas and worked for the *Kansas City Star* or *Times* (Footnote: These newspapers were in Missouri NOT Kansas). Some professors worked as war correspondents or for larger newspapers around the quad state region. Because most professors were Kansas focused, they told students they should expect to work as reporters FIRST and earn their rights to be editors and finally—at a gray old age—they could be publishers for a local small-town newspaper or agriculture magazine. They groomed reporters, writers and editors for Kansas's publications to preserve the regional prairie media trade for the next 100 years.

I was not having any of that. Being born in Kansas was part of a past beyond my control, but dying in Kansas was not part of my future plan. I was NOT going to work at a—as I described it—"small newspaper in Kansas to earn a distinguished place in Kansas newspaper history." Nope. Not me. I was going to be a publisher. There was extreme urgency. Plus, that road had to be streamlined and pure.

So I devised a plan. I figured out early on that the only way I was going to be a publisher before I was 105 was to figure out how to do everything; writing, editing, production, distribution, sales, and even special events. The works. I would learn what I could in Kansas then engineer my escape. I started as a senior in high school. I edited the school newsletter. I wrote and read the weekly St. Xavier news on the local FM station, KJCK (I tried to sound like Barry White delivering the news). I was president of my Junior Achievement company—which received a distinguished achievement award in Kansas City (Missouri). We sold the most emergency car battery lights.

Everything was going my way in college. I was exceptionally mediocre at everything except journalism, psychology and communications courses. I even performed in a student production of Shakespeare's *Comedy of Errors*. A good publisher is a good actor. I established that I could write well. I was a competent reporter. With the help of professors Dave Adams, Bill Brown and Bob Bontrager, I secured two of the most prestigious internships a journalism student could hope for. My junior year I interned with Capital Cities Communications with the *Kansas City Star* (Missouri NOT Kansas). I had multiple front-page features and worked with renowned editor KC Jones and David Zeeck. KC Jones unfortunately passed away many years ago, but Mr. Zeeck and I had a wonderful reunion in 2004. He is now publisher of the *Tacoma Tribune*. During my senior year Dr. Bob Bontrager recommended me for a spot with the *American Society of Magazine Editor's* summer internship program. I won the internship and spent 1980 in New York City at *Fleet Owner Magazine*, a McGraw-Hill magazine on Avenue of the Americas. I worked with another brilliant editor Mike Eigo.

I was now on the cusp of graduating from college, ready to grab my pica pole and take my place in the working journalism world. All I had to do was ace my second *Bowling 101* class and I would graduate with a 2.7 GPA and EXACTLY enough credits to earn my degree. I had experienced a little bit of everything. When not delving in my journalism studies and writing, I excelled in extracurricular activities. Those activities ranged from performing in Shakespeare's *Comedy of Errors*, playing Mr. Scott in the *Not Yet Ready for K-State Players*, working on a crisis line, being a news anchor for the Public TV's *Multicultural Mosaic*, and falling in love once and having my heart ripped out. I wrote a weekly satire column for the *Kansas State Collegian*. I joined a service fraternity Alpha Phi Omega. I was a baker. I sold books door-to-door (*Volume Library Encyclopedia*). I was a burrito maker, a waiter, and perhaps a candlestick maker. I was the consummate collegiate Renaissance man.

I had survived four years without so much as having to lift a calculator. My mathless world was filled with music appreciation, broadcasting, millions of words, bowling and Budweiser. Little did I know that my aspirations to be a publisher would stand a righteous test a few months before graduation. One professor would make a choice to dash or encourage my career goals with his response.

As a senior and consistently average doer, it was a natural and distinctive senior honor to be appointed editor of the journalism department magazine. Part of the job required copy fitting and sizing photos. Both required *the* MATH I had successfully avoided most of my adult life. Producing the magazine required competent use of layouts, a pica pole and a proportion wheel. We were short-staffed, so I was the one who had to do it. One day I was sitting in the magazine production room feeling very frustrated. All the copy for the magazine was edited and corrected, but I just sat staring at the stacks of articles and blank layout sheets. The only word that was now swirling through my head was MATH! MATH! MATH! I couldn't breathe. I was hyperventilating. I reached for a newspaper, separated a section and fashioned a paper bag to try to regulate my breathing. At the very moment, Dr. Bontrager, my advisor, stepped into the room.

"Quinton, are you okay?" he asked, concerned that I may be ill.

Surprised, I lowered the bag and said, "Oh, Dr. Bontrager. I'm okay.

"How's the layouts going?"

"Um, well, I don't know. Everything is edited. Looks good, but I, um, well, I don't know." I stuttered.

Dr. Bontrager pulled out a chair and sat in front of me. Dr. Bontrager was a professor of few words. He spoke precisely, the same way he wrote.

"Come on Quinton, spit it out."

"Well, I don't get this copy-fitting thing," I admitted. "Math stresses me out."

Bontrager laughed. It was one the few times he actually laughed out loud. Mostly he smiled and peered through lightly tinted, thick, Roy Orbison style glasses. Bontrager was in his fifties, partially balding and if he weren't a brilliant instructor he could have been a great Mafia boss. You know the kind of Mafia boss I'm talking about. The kind that quietly says, "I like you Quinton. You make me laugh. But I'm gonna have to kill you anyway. It makes me sad but it's the right thing to do."

"All right, Quinton, let's take it from the top. Grab your pica pole and your proportion wheel…"

I thought about the song I had made up and smiled. Dr. Bontrager walked me through the process, page by page, article by article. He was succinct, spoke clearly and methodically. At first, all I heard was *blah, blah, blah, blah, blah*. After he finished explaining, I look at him with blurred eyes and sweat forming above my brow.

"I still don't understand. How much is pica again?"

Dr. Bontrager smiled and started from the beginning. A pica is…"

Dr. Bontrager kept doing this until the entire magazine was copy fitted and laid out. I kind of got it after that.

I never forgot that moment. I graduated with a degree in journalism and mass communication thanks to Dr. Bontrager and many other great professors at KSU. I was ready to be a publisher. I spent my last summer working at Raul's Escondido making burritos and socking away money so I could go somewhere—anywhere—in the fall.

One day I got a call from fellow journalism graduate Sally Hofmeister. She wanted to have lunch. We met the next day at the Little Apple deli in Aggieville. I liked Sally a lot. She was smart and pretty, with brilliant blue eyes, a cute gap in her front teeth and flowing blonde hair. If she didn't make it in journalism, she could always be a move star.

"What have you been doing since graduation?" Sally asked.

I sipped on my soda and said, "Well, I'm still working at Raul's pushing burritos. I'm socking away my cash so I can go somewhere."

"Where are you going?"

"I don't know. I haven't figured that out yet. What about you?"

Sally hesitated, sipped her coffee, then said, "Well, I'm thinking about going to New York. You worked there last summer. Did you like it?"

"Yep. I did. I adapted. I walked fast everywhere, talked like I knew what I was saying. I wore suits everyday and I always watched my back when I got off the #7 line in Queens," I said. "*And* I lost my obligatory $40 bucks in three-card Monty on Fifth Avenue."

Sally laughed. She had a smile that reeled you in and assured you life was good. If anybody could rule the world with a smile, it was Sally. She didn't say anything for a minute, then stared at me like she was trying to read my mind.

"So, I'm going to New York in September. Do you want to help me drive there? Maybe we can find an apartment together."

My eyes lit up. "Whoa," I said, "That sounds very cool. I thought about going back but wasn't sure. I don't know. I just haven't thought it all the way through yet."

Of course, I loved Sally. Not in a relationship way. Sally was honest. She was always challenging me in the newsroom because we had a mutual respect for each other. She's the only peer who ever said, "Why are you wasting your talents on writing these crazy columns. You can do so much better than this." She had a point. We had a falling out…for a few hours over her criticism. When we reconciled, we were even better friends after that. So much so that I would consider spending a few days in a car driving across country with her; possibly even living together in New York. I was honored.

After some discussion of logistics, I said, "Okay, Sally, you are an amazing editor and human being. You're going to do great in New York, and I think we would survive a road trip without killing each other. Thank you for asking me. I'll have to think about it though."

"Okay, Ray," she said. I let some friends call me Ray if I thought they meant it. "I'm leaving before fall semester starts in late August. Let me know."

"Okay, Sally," I will. We hugged. That was the last time I saw Sally for 25 years. I declined her offer. She drove to New York and landed a gig with the *Wall Street Journal*. Our reunion was in 2005 at a

New Year's Eve party in Sally's Los Angeles home. We were both divorced. She left New York to take a job as features editor of the *Los Angeles Times*, and I was living in Portland, Oregon and publisher of a small newspaper group I founded in Portland and Seattle called the *Lunch Times*. I stayed at her house after the party, and on January 1, 2006, we nursed our hangovers with Champagne and Belgian waffles.

The fall of 1981 was key decision point for me. Sally had gone east and I decided to go west, hoping to eventually get to California. In September 1981, I took a Greyhound bus to Denver. I took up temporary residence with my sister. She loaned me her red Volkswagen Beetle so I could get to interviews. I was forced to park the Beetle blocks away from any interview locations because the front end was pushed to one side because of a massive accident. From the front, it looked like the Bug should have been turning left all the time. I didn't want to scare prospective employers in remote office parks in the suburbs. I quickly landed a job as a unit supervisor with Allstate in an office park way out in the middle of bumfuck nowhere. After a disastrous 6-month stint as a supervisor, I quit, moved out of my condo, got a temp job as a librarian for Chevron and started my first magazine, *Rabid City Humor Magazine* (registered with the Library of Congress) in a rooming house in Capital Hill.

I moved into a studio behind the Bombay Club and secured a regular Friday happy hour gig playing jazz piano to feed my creative music soul. The three-year run of *Rabid City Humor Magazine* (one of the original zines) sealed the mythology of Buddy F. Yutzman. I continued with the quarterly publishing parties And, there are many stories to share about writing, acting, AND music. My drive to be a publisher was fueled by the quest to explore ideas, art, music, culture and humor. And, that I did. It began in Denver and continues to this day. Every day I wake up, grab my pica pole and sing this familiar song to the tune of *Make Them Laugh*:

Grab your pica pole young man and Beeee a publisher.
With your pica pole in hand Beeeee a publisher.
Dance your way into fortune and fame.
Your proportion wheel will show you the game.
Be a publisher!
Be a publisher!
Be a publisher today!

Chapter 13
Writing In My Sleep

I can write in my sleep. I know what you're thinking. "Sure pal, and I can sing like Sanatra." I kid you not. And, rest assured that this is not a false claim from another episode of *Unsolved Mysteries*. I have witnesses and proof.

But first let's digress. Years earlier I set out on a quest to be a publisher. That was 1976. This story picks up 12 years later in 1988. In 12 years I learned everything I needed to be a publisher. Reading, writing, editing, production, photography, distribution, advertising and sales. You name it. I was even a master copy-fitter thanks to Dr. Bontrager and Sally Smith, managing editor at Ortho Books. Both encouraged me to never give up. On Thanksgiving day, for example, I single-handedly copy fitted over 30 cookbooks, including several written by famed cookbook writer Janet Fletcher. Fletcher would later feature my restaurant guide in her food column in the *San Francisco Chronicle*.

I was on top of the world; a bona fide, professional editor and publisher. I was living in a fabulous city. I was partner/Vice-President of Guide Publishing Group, founder and editor of the *Bay City Guide*, executive editor and founder of the *Commercial Property Guide* and managing editor of the *San Francisco Rental Guide*. I had written, edited and published one of the most popular restaurant guide books in San Francisco, *The Afternoon Guide to Lunch In San Francisco's Financial District*, and I was founding editor of one of the most popular restaurant guide in San Francisco.

I was producing massive volumes of copy every month for four different publications. My partner and I had a small staff on the top floor of a Victorian office building on Union Street. My quest to learn and do everything related to publishing was a reality. We owned and managed one of the most successful publishing groups in San Francisco. I was 28. My partner Drew was 29. We didn't care what anyone thought. We just did what we loved to do. publish magazines Out publications made a respectable profit every month after salaries and expenses. We had unlimited access to the arts, events. We could eat at some of the best restaurants on our massive trade accounts. We rented yachts for holiday cruses on the Sacramento River and sailed the bay on weekends on 60-foot sailboats. Our lives were charmed.

As chief writer, editor, photographer, my job included writing event blurbs, feature stories, commercial building profiles and a monthly real estate column for the *Commercial Property Guide*. During production week, we worked long hours, sometimes 18 to 20 hours a day. We produced the magazines on a bank of Mac Pluses and laser printers. We cut and pasted all the copy with Exacto knives and pasted them on mechanical boards using spray-mount, a noxious product that sometimes made us sleepy and a little loopy when we were on a 48-hour production bender. Then we drove the boards to the printer when we finished.

We were due to deliver the boards the next day when we settled into the final leg of our multi-day production cycle for the *Bay City Guide*. I was going through press releases for art openings and writing blurbs (early blogs). After going out to Margaritaville for a nightcap and a chat, we hit the coffee. The office had multiple small rooms with networked computers. I was in one room and Drew was in the other. Sometimes the only way to know there were others in the office was to listen for the clicks of the keyboard. The keyboards for the Macintosh computers were clunky and loud and could easily be heard from one room to the other. Drew was doing past-up in the kitchen and I was feeding him copy from the other room. When I finished a page, I sent it via network to the laser printer next him at the production table. He pasted it up and started on the next page in the tray. If I fell behind, he was left with no copy to past up.

Drew noticed that my delivery of pages was getting slower and slower as the minutes went by. He listened intently to hear the keyboard. When he heard it, he waited for the next page. If I took too long, Drew would get anxious.

"Hey, Ray!" he would yell. "How's it going?"

"Great!" I would say immediately, "We're getting close."

We were both in publisher's heaven. The Macintosh was a miracle machine for publishers. In Denver, to typeset my Zine, I typed columns with a manual typewriter and cut them out. At Ortho Books I used their massive Atex systems that required mainframes and IT people. The Macintosh changed all that. Drew and I could produce three magazines in a week with just five people and four computers. Overnight, we could compete with all the established publications in town for a fraction of the costs.

We used PageMaker 1, Microsoft Word, and manipulated images with PhotoShop to create print-ready halftones. I wrote, edited, then designed the page, inserted formatted images and proofed the pages before I sent them to Drew. The volume of work was massive. But it was the most fun we ever had. Somehow we kept producing day and night until every article was written, edited, produced in PageMaker and pasted up.

Around 3:30 a.m. Drew heard my typing slowing down. Then the sounds stopped.

"Hey, Ray! You awake!" he yelled.

The typing started up immediately. "Yep! Got another page coming your way!" I yelled.

"Okay. Thanks Ray. The pages look good. We're almost done."

Another hour went by. It was 4:30 a.m. and we were delirious with exhaustion. But we kept going. We were operating on pure adrenaline and the excitement of finishing the issues. We usually had some music playing to keep us pumped up as well; maybe some Kenny G or Sade, that was all the rage at the time.

At some point, Drew turned the music down and just listened to my fingers typing. He got excited when we started to notice an unusual patter.

Whenever a new page was sent to print, my typing started out fast and furious as I worked on new blurbs. As the minutes progressed, my typing slowed to a snails crawl. Then, there was a gap where I proofed the page and sent it to Drew. Sometimes the typing slowed to a slow methodical punching of keys, not the usual rapid pace. Then, there would be gaps in the typing and the typing would start up rapid fire.

We finished around 6 a.m. Drew and I fetched the company van and drove the mechanical boards to Alonzo's Press in South San Francisco. We were giddy and tired and proud. Mr. Alonzo loved to see us. The monthly press run of all of our publications combined was over 300 pages and over 100,000 publications in circulation. We were publishing dynamos and were having the time of our lives. Next stop was breakfast. My favorite place was Lori's Diner in Union Square. We drove back to San Francisco and found our favorite corner booth with the view of Union Square. I ordered my usual steak and eggs. Drew ordered the big scrambler and we drank regular rounds of coffee. After breakfast it would be time to go home and go to bed.

Halfway through our breakfast, Drew looked at me, smiled and said, "Hey, Ray, Guess what you were doing last night?"

I stopped eating and looked at Drew. I didn't now what he was getting at.

"We worked our asses off," I said.

"Well, yeah, that's true," Drew said. "But, you did something different. Something I've never seen before."

He didn't elaborate. He just grinned like he'd won the lottery or figured out where Jimmy Hoffa's body is buried.

"Stop teasing me, smart guy. Tell me what you're getting at."

"Well, Ray, I hate to tell you this. And, I have no idea how you do it. But, you were writing in your sleep."

"Get the fuck out of here! I said," perhaps a little too loud. I glanced around at the disapproving stares from the family next to us. I lowered my voice.

"You're shitting me."

"I kid you not, Ray," Drew said, sounding both astounded and proud to have exposed this phenomenon.

"What the hell are you talking about?"

"Well, I noticed a pattern in your typing last night. Never paid much attention before. But, right after you sent a page to me, your typing was strong and steady. After a few minutes, it tapered off to a slow and steady *TICK, TICK, TICK*, until the pages were done. Sometimes I'd call and your typing sped up again, then tapered off to a *TICK, TICK, TICK*. Last night, I finally investigated without calling your name. And sure as shit, you were fast asleep, sitting straight up, eyes turned up into your brain, sawing logs and typing blurbs."

"What?! How do you know I was typing anything legible,"

"Because I recorded it." His mischievous grin expanded even more.

"You didn't!"

"Yep, I did. Did a close-up of the screen and sure as shit, you were writing in your sleep. Must have memorized what you wanted to write and put your brain on autopilot. Funniest damn thing I ever saw. Especially the spit slobbering out of your mouth and your eyes turning up into your head like you've been possessed by devil or something."

I scratched my head and thought back on the night. I was a too delirious from exhaustion to remember everything. I did recall what could have been gaps in my memory. I didn't remember sleeping, but didn't really remember being awake. It could have been combinations of spray mount high, the margarita and exhaustion.

We had a good laugh AND I demanded to see the tape. We had an even bigger laugh when Drew fired up the VCR at the office the next day and played the short tape. Sure as I'm sitting here, I wrote three blurbs, snoring and bobbing my head in between. Ms. Landry would be proud. I had mastered the art of sleep writing. I imagined her saying to me, "And one day, Quinton, when you have reached writing level eight thousand infinity, you will be able to write in your sleep."

It's 2017 now and Drew and I are still friends. Drew comes to Portland to visit his daughter, my step-niece Zoe, every now and then. She's in her 30s and works at Bridgetown Brew Pub. That's our designated reminiscing place. Usually after a few micro-beers the conversation inevitably rolls around to 1988.

"Hey, Ray," do you remember when you were writing in your sleep?"

Chapter 14
Last Writes or Go Towards the Write

The death of my father and grandmother shortly after graduation from high school made me keenly aware of my own mortality. These two events prompted me to make a pact with death. Since I didn't know when it was going to happen, I was going to tease it a little. I would produce more copy more quickly than one human possibly could. I would write things no human had ever thought of writing. I would treat my friends like royalty and have a party every quarter to celebrate being alive. I would drink as much as I wanted and still be functional. If I made it to age 30, I would welcome death at any time because I would have produced more words than any other human alive and my friends and I would have had the frikin' time of our lives!

Some might describe my plan as attempting to write myself to death. It's an interesting paradox. I wasn't necessarily self-destructive. I wasn't necessarily aloof or detached. Quite the opposite. I was amenable to everything, exclusive to no-one, accepted all people and cultures and sexes and races. The idea that this was my one shot to appreciate every situation I found myself in and all the people within them motivated that acceptance. There was no time to be sexist, racist, bigoted or narrow minded thinking about anything. I didn't want to go to heaven because that sounded dull, and I didn't want to go to hell knowing I had been a mean person. If I could have sex every now and then, that would be okay with me. But, sex was rare and relationships even rarer. I was prepared for that. I spent many long hours practicing being a single, sex-insecure, "self" satisfying artist before I graduated high school. Masturbation was like Yoga for me, and I took it seriously. Often times my practice would be interrupted by my mom pounding on the bathroom door looking for her JC Penny Catalog. One day she confronted me and asked me why the ladies bra section pages were stuck together. I shrugged my shoulders and said, "I dunno."

In 1981, I was the elusive publisher of *Rabid City Humor Magazine*. I created multiple fictional characters to play out all my crazy fantasies and ideas. By day, I was a mild-mannered geological librarian working for Chevron on Colorado Boulevard. When 4:30 came around, I shed my glasses, like Superman and became magazine publisher Buddy F. Yutzman, who was kind of an asshole publisher who was Raymond Quinton's boss. I was Raymond Quinton, the editor, who dealt with real people, which included advertisers, subscribers, and writers and events. But, Buddy was always interfering. Yes, this goofy little magazine had paid subscribers, advertisers, a writing staff, and a multimedia staff. Most people, including my co-workers at Chevron, didn't know I was the mastermind and chief writer. I did most of the illustrations and created pompous characters like Norbert Weiner, the smartest man on the planet. My writer co-conspirator, Lawrence Pryor, wrote such classics as *Bruce Why: Interrogatory Spy* and *Mannequin Depressive*. The goal was to create caricatures of people from my imagination and give them life, voice and ongoing stories. It was my idea of a printed sitcom soap opera that culminated after 4 years with the production of a video called *Buddy F. Yutzman is Missing* and a massive going away party for me in December of 1984 at *Acapella's Restaurant*.

The video was a parody of the game show called *Name that Celebrity* and featured an 8-year-old girl, a woman, and my sister all claiming to be Buddy F. Yutzman. I was the game show host and Ken Hamblin, Jr., son of the famed conservative talk show host Ken Hamblin Senior, was the producer. This was my last Denver project. I had already given notice at Chevron, cashed in my stock, and made my reservations on *Peoples Express*. I purchased a ticket to London on a self-imposed sabbatical. I will detail that time more in Book II, *The Jolly Pre-San Francisco British Period*.

In 1990, I turned 30. My quest to write my self to death had failed. I had written AND edited millions of words. I'd beaten my copy fitting phobia and during the fall of 1986—in one week alone—single-handedly laid out and copy-fitted 30 cookbooks, sized and fit 300 photos, all before going to have Thanksgiving dinner at a little sleepy diner on Haight street called Nikki's Barbecue. I was a copy-fitting animal. I had harnessed the ability to write in my sleep. I was an editor by day and restaurant reviewer by lunch and night. I visited and reviewed over 300 restaurants in the financial district, published a book which became a best selling lunch/restaurant guide, a favorite of famed *Chronicle* Columnist Herb Caen. I was on the A-list for events such as the re-opening of the *Paramount Theatre* in Oakland and the *Orpheum* in San Francisco. PR and marketing reps invited me to all-expense paid events at places like the *Fairmont Hotel*, where I saw Cab Calloway, drank champagne and ate prime rib.

To top things off, I grew weary of drinking. Alcohol just made me tired and the headaches had gotten old. Drinking, as you know, can be very painful; the equivalent of running headfirst into a brick wall on purpose. I mostly gave up drinking after a 70s birthday party at Ray's bar. My bankruptcy was going really well. I had been Vice-President of Guide publishing group, founder of the cities best, widely distributed visitor guide, founder and executive editor of the *Commercial Property Guide* and managing editor of the *Rental Guide*. When I left the Guide Publishing Group, I started a *Seminar Guide* and published that for a year while and did some fun publishing projects for friends, including a poetry book. Then, when I got bored with that, I landed a gig as a production editor with Bancroft Whitney. While working at Bancroft Whitney, I was asked to publish a men's resource magazine called *Quest* to support the burgeoning men's movement. I seemed to be maturing. And as sure as I'm sitting here, I wasn't dead yet. Time for a new plan.

This was the new plan: Write a relationship handbook, meeting my first wife, getting married at San Francisco's City Hall, having one last amazing party at Gio's Restaurant, having my first daughter, then ultimately cashing out my 401K, quitting my job, packing up the family and driving to the lesser-expensive Portland, Oregon.

That's where the next chapter continues. That was 1992. I had made it to thirty plus two plus. I had no choice. I had only written a fraction of what I was destined to write. I had no choice but to recommit—like second round life-venture capitalist financing—to at least the next 30. The rest, as they say, is yet to come.

Portland was and is a strange land in a strange time. Compared to San Francisco it was like the land time forgot. I was excited…and a little scared. We set up roots in a little house in Northeast Portland. I pulled out my Remington Noiseless and started furiously writing the next chapters of my life. All was going well until the sound of the noiseless typewriter awoke my sleeping child. My then and future ex-wife peeked her head in the bedroom/office and said, "You know, we do have a Mac Plus with a 20 gig hard drive and Pagemaker 2. If you use the keyboard, maybe the baby will take her nap."

"Oh," I said, "I guess, I can use that." I smiled, looked at Emilia propping her head up like a cute little pointy-head bobble-head doll, drooling on herself on the bed, and looking as cute as a button. I grabbed my keyboard, winked at young Emilia and typed, "It's not time to write into the light yet…TO BE CONTINUED."

BONUS CHAPTER
EPILOGUE DEDICATION TO
CALVIN RANSOM

Jiggaboos, Big Bands and Gangster Parties
Fall 1978 – Kansas State University

By
Raymond F. Quinton

Sunday night in our Manhattan, Kansas, house was pasta night. After a long week of classes and stress, Calvin Ransom and I would get a bottle of good wine and all the supplies we needed to cook for two, three or more. We sometimes bought a new record or two to play while we cooked, usually jazz-fusion like Jeffrey Lorbor or George Benson. For two poor Kansas State University students, we always ate well.

Calvin did most of the cooking and I did most of the talking. I blabbed on about people, politics and places. It was November and a chill had settled into Manhattan, Kansas. We were on the tail end of beautiful fall and heading into a normal, stark, cold, sometimes-brutal, Kansas winter.

We lived in the ground floor flat of a large old house just west of campus. It came complete with a fireplace, carpeted large living room, and two hardwood-floored bedrooms furnished with some impressive antiques. The kitchen was large and bright with lots of room for gatherings and cooking.

The record player was nestled on one of the built-in shelves in the living room and was wired to speakers in the kitchen. Al Jarreau's *Live* album was the top jazz album in the fall of 1978 and played over the speakers as we started preparing our Sunday meal.

A large pot of spaghetti sauce simmered on the stove as Calvin fussed over it, tasting it periodically. I sat at the table talking. Calvin glanced away from the pot on occasion to acknowledge and comment on something I said, but always re-focused his attention quickly on the pots. He was like a bee, buzzing over a flower; tasting and stirring and adding spices. The fan above the stove hummed and steam glazed the windows and warmed the room as we talked and laughed.

Suddenly, a funny, bizarre thought came to me and I blurted out, "Hey Calvin. I got a question."

I waited for Calvin to respond before I continued. Calvin knew this was my usual segue into something serious, so he obliged me with an appropriate response.

"What Raymond?" he asked, smiling and glancing at me. He knew something outrageous was coming. We had gotten to know each other's queues after living together for four months.

"You know those Warner Brothers cartoons with the Africans dancing around a pot with the white hunters boiling in them?"

This caught Calvin's attention. He stopped, looked at me and smiled,

"Yeah, you mean the ones with the jiggaboos?"

"Yeah, yeah, you know the ones where they be dancing to that jiggaboo jungle music?" We both laughed.

Calvin put his spoon down and proceeded to demonstrate, throwing his arms up in the air, squatting up and down and dancing around the kitchen.

"This what you mean?" he asked.

"That's it!" I yelled, pointing, "They be dancing and singing in harmony 'bout how they gonna eat Livingston."

"They got bones in their hair, big white lips, black as night faces and other crazy shit like that?"

"Yep," I said, "and they always eating watermelons too and everybody knows ain't no watermelons in Africa."

"Thas right," Calvin said, "so what makes you think about that?"

"Lookin' at you, bro…little Negro with those big African lips," I said.

"No you didn't just say that? Did You?!" he said

"Yep, but you know I love you bro. I'm just thinking about those racist characters," I said, "AND I'm thinking about the music they played. That was some bad ass big band music that played in those scenes, racist and all. I wonder who the bands were?"

"You know what," Calvin said, "I've thought about that. We grew up seeing that shit and I remember the music. I'm also embarrassed to think that I thought that shit was funny when I was younger."

"I know," I said, "White folks so good at demoralizing the Negro that even Negroes thought it was funny."

"Well," I said, "It's 1978 and we're getting hip to that shit. BUT, I want to know more about that music. That's the hippest dance music I ever heard. So, I'm going to do some research. Maybe we can have a party or something featuring that kind of music."

Calvin thought for a minute, then said, "You may be on to something. I'd be hip to that."

We had a fantastic dinner that evening. We listened to Grover Washington, George Benson and the Crusaders for the rest of the night…then retired to our rooms and got ready for a busy week. For Calvin, architecture required him to do multiple all-nighters every week. I was studying journalism and for some reason got talked into taking a part in the student production of Shakespeare's *A Comedy of Errors* after I auditioned for a story. So, I was starting dress rehearsals, working at Swanson's Bakery and writing for the student newspaper between classes.

When I had free time, I went to the library and started researching jiggaboo music. It didn't take long to get on the right track. I found the Duke Elington and Count Basie collections. I was getting close. I fell in love with the music. I was hooked. Most wasn't the Jiggaboo music I was looking for. I dug a little deeper. Then, one day I found an album by Chick Web. I thought it was another dead end until it started playing it. And, there it was. I yelled, "jiggaboo!" in the library. If I weren't in a listening room, I would have turned a lot of heads and probably gotten kicked out.

But, there it was; the music I was looking for. Chick Web's album featured an 18 year old Ella Fitzgerald singing *A Tisket a Tasket*. I learned the Chick web schooled Benny Goodman, Duke Ellington and some of the greatest big band leaders on how to really swing. Web was the real king of swing. This was the music black folks danced to in the black clubs that we never heard about. And, this was also the music they used for the racist cartoons. This was exactly what I was looking for. The trail led me through a fascinating musical journey that included Fats Waller, Harry James, Benny Goodman, Count Basie, Billy Eckstein, and some of the greatest big band music I ever heard.

That Sunday at dinner Calvin and I listened to Fat's Waller's *Your Feets Too Big* and mixed in some Mary Lou Williams and Jelly Roll Morton.

"You know, Calvin," I said, "This search has opened my eyes. Did you know that Merrie Melodies made a cartoon called *Snow Black an de Seeben Dwarfs?*

"No shit!" said Calvin, genuinely shocked. "What the hell is that all about?"

"Yep," Hollywood was having a grand laugh at the expense of black folks. It wasn't enough for them that we was enslaved for hundreds of years. They actually kept on displaying us as lesser humans and jokes in cartoons."

"I'll be damned," Said Calvin.

"So, I got an idea."

"Nothing new about that," said Calvin as he shot me a sly smile.

"So, we black and we've got to take back this music and celebrate the genius of these musicians. We gotta have a party of some type featuring this music. What do you think?" I asked.

"You know, I've always been into the gangster movies. Ain't no black folks in those gangster movies. It would be cool and funny if two bruthas put on a gangster party here at Kansas State. I think we can have some fun with that."

"I think you're right. I know all the music from that time now, and you know that gangster thing. Plus, you got a great yellow gangster hat," I said.

"Check this out, Raymond. Not too far away in Kansas City was the Kansas City Massacre and Chicago had the St. Valentine's Day Massacre," Calvin said, getting a little more animated.

He stood up, rubbed his chin and said, "Are you thinkin' what I'm thinkin?"

"YEP!" I said, "A St. Valentine's Day Massacre right here in de house in Kansas!"

"With real jiggaboo music and dancing and shit like that! We will celebrate the African American big band greats and real swing music."

"Yeah, buddy, we bring big band back to life right here in the house."

We were both excited about the idea. But, we had to finish up the semester; classes, work, Shakespeare. The semester ended. The snows came, and we had the break to rejuvenate and refresh. Calvin went home to St. Louis for a few weeks, and I stayed in the house feverishly collecting music. I listened to everything; Benny Goodman, Duke Ellington, Harry James, Frank Sanatra. It was a journey of discovery. Then, when Calvin got back, we listened to the cassette tapes I made and we danced around the house…mimicking the Negro characters from the old racist cartoons. If we couldn't laugh about that kind of racism, we thought, we would end up crying.

February 14 rolled around quickly. To add to the allure, we invited a few other friends to host the party with us, and we all gave each other spoof gangster names. My name was Quintonelli. Calvin's name was Calvonelli. Brad's name was Bradonelli. Thad's name was Thadonelli. Yes, very original.

The party was a hit. Close to 200 people dressed in their vintage gangster outfits showed up. Flapper dresses were in style and everybody danced because the music was the swingingist big band music of all, especially the Chick Web.

Calvin and I got separate apartments the following year, but the gang held together, and we hosted a gangster party every year on St. Valentine's day from 1978 through 1981; with the crowds getting bigger and bigger. The parties became even classier and more legendary every year.

But, it doesn't end there.

I moved to San Francisco in 1985. That same year I revived the tradition of the annual St. Valentine's Day Massacre party in downtown San Francisco. These were the days before the Internet. Calvin and I had lost touch. After two years of hosting the gangster party in downtown San Francisco at some fantastic locations, including the Temple Bar and Grill, a historic speakeasy (in an Alley) and seeing 300 plus people attending, I didn't realize that Calvin had moved to Oakland years earlier. I was walking down Market Street one day when I saw a familiar set of bright eyes, tight trimmed beard and energetic gait.

"Hey, Calvin!" I yelled.

He did a double take, smiled the biggest smile I've ever seen and said, "Hey, Quintonelli. What's Happening!?"

It seemed our destiny was to re-connect and share more of our lives again. We met each other's spouses and children and were reminded that there is such a thing as destiny, joy and love. Calvin was older than I was. He was a great friend, mentor and all around optimist. Optimism gives us strength to pursue and appreciate all the good things in life. Cancer claimed his physical body last year, but I still see him every day. Thank you Calvin. I love you and miss you. You're still here with me every day of the year, especially when I go on Youtube and binge watch those old cartoons and listen to those cats really swing in the background.

My name is Raymond. I'm a writer and I lie like a rug. But, this is a true story about my dear friend and Alpha Phi Omega brother, Calvin Ranson. He is missed.

Raymond Quinton (Quintonelli)

PREVIEW: BOOK#2

INTRODUCTION

1) Smells Like Envy (Did Someone Say They Were a *Successful* Writer?)
2) Write Like You Drive – The Life of A Reckless Writer
3) Cover Letters: I Don't Want Your Job. I Just Like Writing Cover Letters
4) Every Day is a Great Day to Be a Writer
5) See Attached – Blue Collar Writing – Or, Writing Too Much All The Time For Everything
6) Who Was Buddy F. Yutzman
7) Why Writer's Commit Suicide: The Sound of Bees and Mosquitoes
8) Inside Book Awards
9) Stick To Your Own Race – What Color Is Your Character
10) Writer Rock Stars – Why I Want to Be a Dr. Michael Eric Dyson Roadie/Groupie
11) Music In Writing
12) Outlaw Writers
13) Internet Dating – How to Juggle 10 Chats At One time
14) Real Fake Internet Profiles – How Rich People are Gaming the System
15) Fast Food Restaurant Reviews – McDonald's & Others Fine Restaurants – My Years as Publisher *of The Seattle & Portland Lunch Times Newspapers*
16) Empathic Advertising Sales
17) AND MORE!

Publisher's note: With the publishing of book #1, I will start working on book #2 in this series immediately. I'll revisit <u>Rabid City Magazine</u> *in Denver then take you on a ride through the 90s and the 2000s. There will be three books all told. So, fasten your seat belt and enjoy the ride. Above are some samples of chapter titles.*

Made in the USA
Middletown, DE
22 June 2024